Shaken, Broken and Reborn

Lorita Kelsey Childress

Noire Passion is an imprint of Parker Publishing Inc

Published by Parker Publishing Inc
12523 Limonite Avenue, Suite #440-176
Mira Loma, California 91752
www.parker-publishing.com

ISBN: 978-1-60043-167-8 (print)
First Edition

Manufactured in the United States of America
Cover Design by Parker Publishing Inc

"Lorita Kelsey Childress has done it again! Shattered Broken and Reborn is an amazing read and page turner. The take away message from this book is at your lowest point; God can come in and turn this around so fast it will have your head spinning." - Jahzara Bradley, Author of Love Don't Live Here Anymore.

"Lorita Kelsey Childress has the ability to capture a reader with the first sentence. The attention to detail allows you to be drawn into the story and want more. We LOVED this book and thoroughly enjoyed the story. Great job Mrs. Kelsey Childress!" - Reading Sisters, Pittsburgh, PA.

DEDICATION and ACKNOWLEDGEMENTS:

This book is dedicated to my husband, David Carmichael Childress. He is a survivor! I am so blessed to know him, to love him, and to be a part of his amazing journey. He is my rock when I am weak, my comforter when I'm hurting, and the joy that makes my heart beat. I pray our love will be a testament to our children, grandchild, family, and friends. "Wherefore they are no more twain, but one flesh. What therefore God hath joined together, let not man put asunder," (Matthew 19:6, KJV).

Prologue

What do you look forward to at the end of your long hectic workday? If you are anything like me, I'm sure most of you would probably love to come home to an empty house and just relax. No kids running around the house asking you for this or that. You can just sit back and unwind in the tranquility of your home. This is the time of day you look forward to, that you deserve.

Well, that's the point I am in my life. I have four beautiful children or should I say young adults. All of them are out of the home trying to make their way in this crazy unpredictable world.

My youngest daughter Lorna is eighteen. She just graduated from high school and is off to Claflin University, in South Carolina.

Lorna has always had goals and aspirations. She has already decided to become a pediatrician. Lorna is very ambitious. She wants to open an office in the inner city so she can provide the best possible care for those who are less fortunate.

Lorna is the nuttiest of all my children. The jokes she used to tell when she was younger were by far the stupidest jokes you ever did hear. I'm telling you, sometimes she was the only one laughing but hey she was always a happy child.

Then there is my youngest boy, twenty year old, Isaiah. In his mind he is the finest thing walking around on this earth. Now, don't get me wrong he is a very attractive, well built young man but he's just got his priorities in the wrong place. Isaiah believes the world owes him everything and anything his heart desires. Isaiah feels he can get what he wants in life from the women who seem to fall down at his feet. Young and old women love them some Isaiah.

He truly believes his manhood is based on how many women he can woo in a day. I'm telling you the boy has some serious issues. If you are a mother, I am sure you can relate and appreciate where I am coming from when I tell you there's always one child in the bunch who you worry about more than the others. I have taken Isaiah to the altar on several occasions. He has a permanent seat in the second pew at Mt. Ararat Missionary Church of God in Christ!

I fear Isaiah's reality check is coming sooner than later. I feel it in my bones. This child really needs a talk with Jesus. Trust me on that one.

Isaiah is attending Morehouse University in Atlanta Georgia, at least for this semester. It's hard to believe he received a full academic scholarship. The boy's grades go up and down like a yoyo because he can't leave those cute girls alone who attend Spellman and Clark Atlanta. I pray he doesn't make me a grandmother before my time. Well, that's all I am going to say about him but you get the picture.

My oldest daughter, Shannell is twenty-two and is attending her senior year at Johnson C. Smith University in North Carolina. I am so proud of her. It took Shannell a while to find her way but she did. All I can say the power of prayer really works.

Shannell during her last year declared she wanted to become a lawyer. Shannell's decision to become a lawyer is the absolute best decision the child has ever made in her life. Becoming a lawyer is the perfect occupation for her.

It seems like yesterday when Shannell learned how to talk, we realized her gift of gab. I swear she would find an excuse, argument, or justification for whatever she was doing. Sometimes she would talk so fast the words rambled together like a train on a collision course. Shannell would try to throw out big words she didn't even know the meaning of. She was always trying to gain the upper hand, using that entire mumble jumble to change the issue or to manipulate the situation while she tried to defend herself or her siblings.

By the time Shannell finished her opening arguments, she had confused the mess out of me. I started believing I was wrong for punishing her. Now, what Shannell could do was an art. Watch out world!

Then there is my oldest boy Clark. He graduated from Howard University in the original chocolate city, Washington, D.C. He is starting his second year of medical school at John Hopkins University, in Baltimore. He is torn between becoming a cardio vascular surgeon or a neurologist.

Clark is twenty-five years old. He is the finest young man I have ever seen if I must say so myself. Now don't think I am perverted or anything. I am just stating the facts. He looks so much like his daddy its ridiculous, right down to his father's deep chocolate skin and his hazel eyes.

Clark is definitely a momma's boy. He almost had a heart attack when he was pledging Omega Psi Phi because he was only allowed him to call home on Sundays. Before he went on line we spoke every day. When he got a chance to call home we would talk for hours.

Clark is a very responsible young man unlike his younger brother. Since the kid's father died when he was eight years old, Clark assumed the role of being the man of the house. Being responsible for your younger siblings and trying to keep your mother from making a mess of her life can make a child old before his time.

Clark is very religious and relies on God to lead him. He doesn't rely on his good looks and charm to get him by. Vanity is not in his vocabulary. I know I am probably showing favoritism. Maybe, it's because I can always count on my boy.

When Clark comes home from college, the phone never stops ringing. All my friends want their daughters to marry my son. To be honest, not one of those girls is good enough for him. They better go look at Isaiah and leave momma's pride and joy alone.

I know that sounded so terrible. I really do love all of my children. I would gladly die if it meant one of them could live. I just love each of them in different ways.

If you would ask one of my children whom I loved the most, each one of them would answer they were number one in my life. Now that's a good thing.

My children have really been a blessing in my life. Not one of them got into drugs or belonged to any gangs. My girls never got an abortion and my sons never fathered any children. Now, that's a miracle in itself. I am forever grateful to my Lord and Savior. Our life has not always been easy but God always provided a way.

As I was saying before I got side tracked about the kids. I am sitting on the couch drinking a tall glass of cranberry juice and munching on some popcorn and that's dinner.

I have my favorite CD cranked up loud and clear. Maxwell is singing the opening line from "Lifetime" it is so powerful. Have you really listened to it? "I was reborn when I was broken…" Maxwell, you ain't ever lied. That line sums up my life.

I am a woman who has been verbally and physically abused. I've also contemplated committing suicide on more than one occasion.

At eighteen, I married my childhood and high school sweetheart, Grant and became pregnant with Clark. By the time, I was twenty-six I suddenly found myself a widower, alone, and left with no family who could or wanted to help me with my children.

At thirty six, I realized I had wasted a decade of my life as I tried to find the next man who would save my life, that man who would rescue me out of poverty, that man who would love me unconditionally, that man who would rock my world, that man who would not cheat on me, that man who would not kick my butt, that man who would be a father to my children.

While I was looking for Mr. Right, dodging bill collectors, and trying to make ends meet, ten years of my children's life flashed before my eyes. I missed the formative years of my children's development. I hate to admit it but I became a part time mother. I was so caught up in my own thing I realized I lost valuable precious time with my children. The funny thing about time, once it's missed it can never be replaced. Time becomes a memory a part of your past.

I got so caught up in the world I lost my self worth, my dignity and my faith. I no longer valued my body, my family, my friends, or my soul. I was lost. It's hard to believe we live in a world of mass destruction, in a world which terrorist could strike at any time and yet I live in a world where the first African American became the forty fourth President of the United States of America.

It took me forty-three years when I realized the devices of the enemy were geared to make me forget from whom my blessings came from. So I turned my life around. I became a living testimony of what God can do in your life. God was and always is the answer. He is the truth and the light. He can set you free from your prison, your hell here on earth.

Today, I am CEO, Founder, and President of Visions of Beauty. Visions of Beauty, is a one hundred- fifty five million dollar a year company, located in the heart of downtown Pittsburgh, Pennsylvania. My company is very unique and it has become the model for other institutions across the country.

Visions of Beauty, is a beautiful facility where women can come and be pampered all day long. It is a hair and nail salon and day spa with a twist. It includes a gym, and a little snack bar which serves juices, fruit smoothies, and low calorie type foods.

After you get pampered you can go upstairs and browse the boutique. The boutique specializes in plus sizes but we have a little something for the undernourished women.

I did not design Visions of Beauty alone. I had some help. God had a plan and He gave me the vision. You see Visions of Beauty also works with the welfare system, especially with the clients of the Welfare to Work program. I donate a full day of pampering to those ladies who have completed the Welfare to Work program. I give them a fresh haircut, beautiful nails, a new suit, and new shoes so they can look their best for their upcoming interviews. They can even work out at the gym. The entire day is free. It is my graduation present to them, for all of their hard work and determination to succeed. Some of my clients, have never been to a beauty parlor, let alone purchased a designer suit.

It is so rewarding to see these women being transformed right before your eyes when they decide to let their inner beauty breakthrough and shine as they start to feel good about themselves. These women leave Visions of Beauty empowered with a positive attitude, feeling they can conquer the world and get that job or anything else they might want out of life.

An African American bookstore is situated in the rear portion of Visions of Beauty. If you are going to be beautiful, you must be educated. Now I'm not saying you have to be a scholar but you should know a little something. Beauty quickly fades and can't pay the bills but knowledge is power it can't be taken away from you and stays with you until the end.

I want all my clients to be knowledgeable so they can get the good jobs to ensure they can take care of themselves and their families. I want them to stay in school because education is one of the keys to life.

Visions of Beauty, is also equipped with seminar rooms. I try to provide speakers who will empower and equip women with hope and guidance. On Wednesday nights, Pastor Rollins from First Baptist holds his Bible study at my facility. You definitely couldn't get anywhere without Him!

God provided and equipped me with His vision. He led me to all the right people and to the right building. He did all of this to make His vision a reality by using me.

Now, don't get me wrong- I wasn't always the religious type. I have had more trials and tribulations than probably some of you have had in a lifetime. I used to fornicate, I spoke using tons and tons of obscenities, and I could gossip. Now, I'm not saying I am perfect I am a work in progress trying to do what God wants me to do. I'm just a sistah trying to do what is right before God calls me home to glory. I desire to meet Him at the pearly gates and hear Him say "Well done, my good and faithful servant well done."

That's why that song hits me. In the midst of all my storms and all of my heartaches I was reborn. Unbeknownst to me God was teaching me, guiding me, preparing me for what I have today. I can now look back over my storms and be thankful for what I have learned, for what I have endured. I believe all of my life lessons have made me in some aspects a better person. I may have been shattered and broken in this journey called life, but deep down in my spirit I was being remolded, reshaped, and reborn.

I've always had some faith. My faith may have been the size of a mustard seed at times but it was enough that I could receive God's grace and mercy. It took me many years to understand that no matter what I have gone through whether it was good times or bad times God was always with me. He carried me when I didn't have a clue. He walked beside me when I was weak.

Like I said before, life wasn't always so pleasant for me. In order for you to understand the ending of my life, you have to start at the beginning. By the way my name is Unique Blackman Johnson. Yes, I said Unique. You see God made me unique right from the start. Well… that's what Momma told me and this is my story.

Chapter 1

I was born Unique Blackman at 6:05 p. m. on June 19, 1959 at Magee Women's Hospital in the city of Pittsburgh. I was the only child of Jenny and Morris Blackman.

I won't bore you with the first years of my life. It's basically a blur. In my opinion, anybody who can tell you what happened to them when they were that young was lying plain and simple. Trust me on that.

For the most part, I knew I was well taken care of and loved by my mother. When you were young that's all that mattered. Basically, you wanted to receive some hugs and kisses, you wanted to play, eat, and sleep. But in an instance, all of that seemed to change…

"Unique! Unique! Damn it! Don't you hear me calling you?"

"Uh… Daddy what's wrong?" I yelled down the hall as I rubbed my eyes and climbed out of my bed.

I slowly walked down the hallway toward the four steps which led to the split level living room. My mother peaked out her bedroom door and screamed at my father. "Really, Morris, it is one o'clock in the morning what could you possibly want Unique to do at this time of night?"

My father's baritone voice vibrated throughout the house. "Go back to bed Jenny! I didn't call you. This doesn't concern you!"

My mother barley uttered, "But…"

My father rotated his neck so quickly I thought it was going to snap as he angled himself so he could get a better view of my mother who was standing in front of her bedroom door. "Shut the fuck up, Jenny, and go back to bed!"

Quickly, he diverted his attention to me. "Unique. Get your mother fuckin' ass down here and change this damn TV channel. Put it on channel two."

I stood at the top of the stairs with a perplexed look on my face. I was still half asleep and in a daze. "Daddy, you woke me up for that? You are sitting right by the TV."

"Girl, don't open up your mouth again. Just get down here and change the damn channel!"

When you're ten years old and its one o'clock in the morning you should be snug in your bed dreaming… dreaming of the Jackson

Five and trying to figure out who you thought was better looking...Michael or Marlon? And was Tito really their biological brother? Instead, I began a slow decent downstairs, as I rubbed the sleep out of the corner of my eyes as I tried to figure out why my Daddy had lost his mind.

At the end of the hallway was my parent's bedroom. Momma was peeping out the door with fright in her eyes. She was petrified. Her face was contorted with fear. It was the face I had seen so many times when Daddy was about to go off on her. It's the look that pleads oh…no…not again. She doesn't speak a word to me but her eyes tell me to shut up and do as I am told quickly, fast and in a hurry.

Daddy was a big politician, a Republican who was very well known throughout the Alleghany County community. All the white people loved him because he was just light enough for their comfort zone but not dark enough to make them feel that they loved black folks. The black people, on the other hand, despised Daddy because to them he was a sell-out.

Momma told me Daddy always struggled with the color of his skin, that he was teased when he was younger and ridiculed as a young man in college. He pledged a black fraternity hoping it would make him feel blacker. She said Daddy never really fit in with black or white people. He felt stuck in the middle of two worlds. After college he decided to blend in with the white race because it was just easier.

To me, it didn't make any sense. How could Daddy ever escape his race? And why would he want to be something he's not? Even his last name reminded him of what he didn't want to be… a Blackman.

Everyone thought my parents were the "ideal" couple. Mom was the devoted, beautiful stay-at-home wife who gave up her career as a Registered Nurse in order to ensure her home was taken care of. I remember sitting in front of the television set watching the soap opera, The Guiding Light as my Mother ironed and starched all of Daddy's shirts. His shirts had to have all the right creases in the sleeves, the collar had to have just the right amount of stiffness. They had to appear crisp and new or there would be consequences to pay. He had a reputation to maintain and my Mother made sure Daddy was always presentable and looked dapper. He didn't believe in taking a bad photograph.

Daddy was the handsome, self-made man who took political chances that most would avoid. He loved controversy. He often told me, "Unique, if people aren't talking about you then you are doing something wrong. In my book there is no such thing as bad publicity."

He put himself through law school and became a brilliant attorney who had enough balls to run for Mayor and won. Morris Blackman became the first African American mayor in the history of Pittsburgh. Some white people refused to believe Daddy was black.

Daddy had many accolades and accomplishments. He worked hard at his political career while diligently keeping up the façade he was providing a warm and loving environment for his lovely wife and adorable daughter. My parents personified the so-called "American dream." Our so-called family was the family that everyone, black or white, wanted to aspire to.

Daddy had many enemies but he didn't let it bother him. He was once quoted in the Pittsburgh Courier, "Enemies are nothing but foot stools to help you climb to the top. If a few get squashed along the way it's not my problem."

Our family's public image was a complete scam. No one knew what went on behind the closed doors of our modest upper middle class home. My Mother and I endured verbal abuse almost on a daily basis. My poor Mother saw Daddy's fist whenever a bad mood struck him.

I never knew if Daddy really loved me. Affection was not in his vocabulary. I felt I was just an infected sore festering in his side until I turned eighteen. I often wondered if he had gotten married and had a family just for show. Were we pawns used to aide his political agenda?

Daddy never showed any warmth towards me. No hugs, no kisses, and no good night stories were read to me as I was tucked underneath my nice warm covers. Not once did my evening end with a loving embrace from my father. I never received any birthday or Christmas presents which he took the time to purchase. My Mother said he loved me in his own twisted bizarre way. She said Daddy always gave her the money to get my gifts or whatever else I needed. My Mother didn't realize what I needed from Daddy money couldn't buy.

Often I felt like I was my Daddy's personal servant. My master rewarded me by providing a roof over my head, food in my belly, and some nice clothes. All I ever wanted was some real love and affection from him. I needed to hear my Daddy tell me he was proud of me, that he loved me, and he was blessed to have me in his life. Isn't a father supposed to do those types of things with his only daughter? Wasn't he supposed to make me feel like his little princess and be the apple of his eye? Wasn't he supposed to be the first man I would love?

At night, I would dream, wishing Michael or Marlon would come and get me up out of my misery and take me back to Indiana.

I could never figure out why my Mother always stuck up for Daddy. She said she didn't have to work and he paid the bills. Mother said Daddy was a good man because he provided for us and sent me to a private school.

How could he be a good man when she saw his fist at least once a week and she was referred to in a derogatory way? And I didn't ask to go to that school with all those snobby rich white kids. Did he care about my feelings? Hell no. Everything my father did was a calculated premeditative move which he planned precisely to ensure he remained politically correct for the white man.

Now my beautiful Mother was the sweetest woman in the world. She was all of five-foot-two and weighed about a hundred twenty-five pounds. Back in the day, she would have been considered a "Brick House". Her eyes were brown with a hint of a red. When they weren't full of tears, they sparkled like diamonds. Her smile was shear radiance which radiated from within her soul and it could warm your heart. My Mother always found a way to turn a bad day into a good day. She once had smooth caramel colored skin but the abusive imprints of my father's fists tarnished it.

I don't know why she stuck with Daddy all those years. I know she could have had any man in the world she wanted. She could have had a man who would have respected and loved her. She needed a man who would call her sweetheart instead of calling her nasty obscenities.

Mother recalled when she was a teenager my Daddy used to work at a butcher shop in the Hill District of Pittsburgh. The shop was on the Center Avenue bus line. She could see Daddy chopping up the meat from the big picture window. Mother and all her girlfriends used to ride the bus back and forth so they could just look at him. Supposedly, he was the best looking boy around the neighborhood. He passed the test. You know that test, lighter than a brown paper bag. Back then, the color of your skin even among black folks was criteria of the upmost importance. He also had the ultimate prize possession, "good hair." With all those attributes, Morris Blackman was every girl's dream.

Mother imagined what their kids would look like. Some dreams should never come to fruition.

I loved my Mother. She was my sister and best friend. She was my protector even when she couldn't protect herself from the blows of my father. Mother prayed for deliverance but it seemed like God didn't want to deliver her. Well, that's the way I saw it. However, deliverance did come for my Mother but it came too soon.

My time with Mother was drastically cut short. Mother died when I was eleven. The doctors said she had an artery which ruptured in her head. I believe that like I believe I can walk on water. In my heart, I know my Mother died from getting whipped by my father's hands. Unfortunately, on numerous occasions my young eyes witnessed my Daddy hitting my Mother upside her head but who was going to prove she was an abused woman? In the seventies that type of stuff you kept quiet. Who would believe she died at the hands of her man especially when her husband was the mayor of Pittsburgh? He was untouchable.

Life ended the day we put my wonderful mother in the ground. Once mother was buried, Daddy started to stay away from home most nights. When he did return home, his abusive behavior was now vented toward me. I became his replacement bitch, the one who would be compelled to keep his dirty secrets.

Chapter 2

Fourteen for me was an awkward age as I was beginning to develop. I started my period, gained some weight, and I began wearing braces. The little self-esteem I had plummeted as pimples populated my face. I was a light skinned girl with nasty puss filled irritants all over my skin. They surely didn't enhance any beauty which was hiding in the background of my maturing face. I felt ugly and unloved.

On a very hot day in July my friends and I were playing hopscotch in front of old Mrs. Frazier's house. Mrs. Frazier was one of our neighbors who had died about two months ago. She was one of the last white people who lived on our block who didn't run and sell their house when they saw the invasion of the upper middle class blacks moving into the neighborhood.

We watched as the realtor pounded the "Sold" post on Mrs. Frazier's front lawn. Everyone in the neighborhood anticipated the arrival of our new neighbors. I hoped for a nice family who had a bunch of girls.

Out of nowhere, a huge moving truck with oversized blue lettering Tri State Movers pulled into old Ms. Frazier's driveway. It caused a ruckus in the neighborhood. The neighborhood became alive as people started opening up their doors and meandered outside so they could get a peak at who it was moving in.

It was rumored the older neighbors had a friendly wager with each other. The bet was simple, no white family would purchase Mrs. Frazier's house because most of the white people had disseminated and moved out of these suburbs. White folks were scurrying like rats as they hurriedly moved to the exclusive rich white neighborhoods of Squirrel Hill, Shadyside, and Fox Chapel as they prayed the Negros wouldn't follow. It would be a travesty if a Negro was rich enough to purchase a home in anyone of those communities.

Well, we won the bet. The Johnsons were black as midnight. There was no mistaking them as white folks.

A red Corvette pulled into the driveway behind the moving truck. I caught a glimpse of the cutest dark skinned boy looking out the window. Oh my goodness, he smiled at me and my heart stopped. The car doors of the red Corvette opened and the boy jumped out. He said something to the shapely woman in the red strapless dress. She patted him on the head and gave him a kiss. The next thing I knew, the boy was coming our way bouncing his basketball. I had no idea my future was heading in my direction.

He was the most handsome dark skinned boy I had ever seen in my life. He had curly dark brown hair which was cut close on the sides. His skin was so smooth he looked like a Hershey's candy bar. When he smiled, my God… he was perfection. I knew he had to brush his teeth at least three times a day. Suddenly, that boy was standing right next to me.

"Hi, my name is Grant."

I had never experienced nerves which over took me. "Hi, my name is Unique."

"Unique?"

"Yes, Unique. You got a problem with that?"

Grant stepped back. "No, it's… it's just, I never met anyone with a name like that before. It's just different, and it's unique."

"Now you've got it. I am Unique."

We both started laughing up a storm while my impatient and jealous girlfriends looked on.

Char cleared her throat before she spoke. "Dag, Unique, aren't you going to introduce us?"

"Sorry, Char. Where are my manners?"

"Grant these are my best friends in the whole world. This is Charlotte. We call her "Char" for short and that pip squeak over there is Ruby."

"Hi, Grant." They said in unison while smiling up a storm.

But Grant hardly paid them any attention. All eyes were on me. For some reason I was tingling inside. What was wrong with me? I could barley speak.

"Grant, where did you move from?"

"Oh, we lived in Oakland not far from the University of Pittsburgh. My dad got a promotion a few months back so he thought we should move to the suburbs. Claims the schools are better."

"Oh…" was all I could say. I felt so awkward. It wasn't like every day I had a cute boy stand in front of me who actually wanted to have a conversation with me. I was invisible to most.

Still bouncing the basketball as he spoke, "You got any brothers or sisters?"

"No. It's just me and my Daddy."

"What about your mother?"

I put my head down and whispered, "She… she died a few years ago."

Grant stopped bouncing the ball and took a step toward me. He gently lifted my chin, and looked deeply into my eyes. "Oh… I'm sorry."

A wave of emotion flooded my body. I stepped backwards and released myself from Grant's tender touch. "Thanks...um, you got any brothers or sisters?"

"Sure do. I have two brothers and a sister they are triplets."

"Wow, Triplets? I have never seen any triplets, well maybe on TV. Where are they? I didn't see them get out of the car. How old are they?"

"The crazy trips are two. They are at my Big Momma's house until we get settled."

Suddenly, a loud rumble came from down the street. "Unique. Get your fast behind in here."

My heart sank. I couldn't believe my Daddy's timing. Of all the days, he picked today to come home early from work. "Coming, Daddy." I was dying with embarrassment.

Grant grabbed my hand as I whizzed by. "Hey Unique, your Daddy looks familiar like I've seen him before. Is he a television star or something?"

Before I could say anything Ruby and Char yelled, "He's the Mayor."

I was so humiliated I wanted to crawl into our infamous potholes. People always treated me different when they found out who my Daddy was.

Daddy's voiced echoed in a thunderous roar throughout the neighborhood. "Unique!"

I snatched my hand from Grant. "Look I got to go. Bye, Grant. See you Ruby and Char."

Ruby yelled as I ran down the street. "Unique, ask if you can spend a night over Char's house I'm going too."

"I will and I'll call you later." I yelled as I feverishly ran down to my house.

"Bye, Unique."

"Bye, Grant."

I ran in the house and closed the door. I almost pissed on myself. Grant had my heart racing.

The next morning and many mornings after our first encounter Grant came down to my house and sat on the front porch. He always waited until he saw Daddy leave for work. I believe Grant was scared of my Daddy, which he should have been. Daddy would kick his butt and mine if he saw Grant hanging around the house.

"No boys, no girls, nobody in our house." Daddy would say every morning before he left the house.

Early in the morning was the only time Grant and I would have time to spend with each other because Char and Ruby would soon be running down the street headed to my house.

As soon as I heard the three taps and a pound on the front door I knew when I opened the door Grant would be standing there flashing his irresistible smile.

"Hey, Unique"

"Hey, Grant"

I came outside and sat on the swing which adorned the front porch as well as two chairs and a chaise lounge. Grant sat beside me and held my hand.

He winked at me. "Is that a new short set?"

"Yes, it is." I said proudly as I got up from the swing and twirled around so Grant could get a good look.

"I like it. The color pink looks really good on you."

I was blushing up a storm and a faint "thank you" escaped my lips.

"Are you anxious for school to start? I heard the school was pretty cool."

I started to fidget in my seat. "I wouldn't know, Grant."

Grant gave me a puzzled look. "You wouldn't know… Are you some drop-out or something?"

A slight laugh escaped me. "No, silly. I go to the all-white prep school on Fifth Avenue."

"Way down there? Why?"

"Because my Daddy wants me to attend there and he pays big money for my education."

"Dag…Unique, I'm disappointed. I was looking forward to seeing you in some of my classes, eating my lunch with you, and maybe sneaking a kiss in the hallway."

Grant leaned over and kissed me right on the lips. At first, I wasn't sure what I was supposed to do. This was a new experience. Grant's warm smooth tongue slipped in and out of my mouth. I felt electric pulsations run throughout my entire body. I was delirious with this newfound feeling of ecstasy. I didn't know a thing about this type of kissing so I just followed Grant's lead. I was on a complete natural high. Grant and I were so engrossed with each other we didn't see or hear Ruby and Char come up to the porch. Out of nowhere, we heard this loud laughter which immediately broke our embrace.

"I'm telling your Daddy." Ruby said while pointing her finger at us.

I quickly wiped my mouth as I tried to regain my composure. I screamed "Shut up, Ruby!"

"How long have you two been standing there?" Grant said as he fidgeted in his seat and placed his hands over the bulge which was pressing against his pants.

"Long, enough," they said in unison.

"Don't worry," Char said. "You can eat lunch with us."

Then rude Ruby bounced her narrow behind over to the swing and wedged herself between Grant and me. She proceeded to remove Grant's hand from his bulge and placed her hands on his private part, saying, "And I'll let you kiss me. You can pretend I'm Unique."

Grant was mortified by Ruby's hand on his hardening member he jumped up and ran up the street to his house. Ruby and Char sounded like a bunch of cackling hens as they stood on my front porch laughing hysterically.

"Grant, wait you forgot your basketball." I yelled up the street while trying not to laugh myself.

You could barley hear Grant as he opened the door to his house. "Keep it I'll get it later." He shouted before he slammed the front door.

The day after Labor Day signaled the start of a brand new school year. Weeks passed by before I saw Grant again. We kept missing each other.

Everyday on his way home from school Grant picked up the triplets from the babysitters and watched them until his parents got home. Then he had to do his homework before he went to basketball practice. Unfortunately, his tight schedule left no time for me.

Ruby and Char took delight in telling me all the girls at school were trying to talk to Grant but he ignored all of them. He barely spoke to them. That bit of news made me feel a little bit better but I still missed my new friend. I wanted to feel more of that feeling, that tingling sensation I felt when Grant kissed me. I never knew my body would yearn for another person's touch. I was experiencing feelings I had no idea if it was okay to feel. Oh how I wish my mother was around. I knew I could always talk to Ruby or Char's mothers but it wasn't the same. What if these feelings were considered dirty or wrong? I would be humiliated and couldn't face their mothers ever again.

I was walking home from the bus stop one afternoon and whom did I see? Grant. He was walking with the triplets. My heart started to race, my feet started running, and my mouth started screaming, "Grant, Grant, holdup."

"Hey, Unique, where have you been hiding?"

I was beaming from ear to ear. "Me? Hiding? You're the one who just ran off weeks ago. Anyway, stop by my house and get your basketball."

"I can't. Besides, I need to get my brothers and sister in the house. It's kind of cold out here."

I looked down at the three curious sets of eyes which were looking up at me. "Hi, kids. Awe…Grant they are so adorable."

Grant's siblings looked at me like I was an alien life form. I know my body is changing but I didn't think I was looking bad. Grant must have felt the uncomfortable feeling that suddenly overtook me because he looked at me and said, "They aren't going to say nothing to you because they don't know you. My parents have drilled it in their heads not to speak to strangers. Don't take it personally."

"Oh…okay. But they are so cute. What are their names?"

"This is Marra, Malcolm, and Marvin."

Before I knew it we were in front of Grant's house.

Grant paused as he let the triplets into the house. "Well, I got to go."

I touched his arm. "Grant, can we just start over? I kind of miss you."

"Maybe."

I felt dejected. "That's it? Well… okay then."

With my head hung low I started walking toward my house.

"Hey, Unique?"

I turned around so fast it's a wonder I didn't get whiplash.

"Yes, Grant?"

"I'll ask my mom but if she says yes, you think your dad would let you come over for dinner?"

"Dinner?"

"Yeah…girl, you heard me. Would you like to come over for dinner?"

"Sure, that would be fun. Call me later."

I was so happy I skipped all the way home. Things were looking better!

Chapter 3

A week later I was in my room studying for a Spanish test and the phone rang.

"Hello, Unique."

"Yeah, this is she. Who is this?"

"Um… this is Grant."

"Sorry, Grant, I didn't catch your voice. It's about time you called me."

"I would have called you sooner but you never gave me your number. Remember, before school started I would just come down your house if I wanted to see you."

"You're right. So how did you get my number?"

"I have my sources."

"Yeah, I bet. Do they go by the names of Char and Ruby?"

Grant and I both busted up laughing.

"You know your girls Unique, they look out for you."

"I know. Char and Ruby are the sisters I never had."

"What are you doing right now, Miss Unique?"

"I'm studying for my first period Spanish test. So Grant, what did you want?"

"I told you I was going to invite you to dinner. My mom said Friday was good and then she would drop us off at the movies. Well, that's if you want to go."

My heart was rapidly beating in my chest. "Grant, are you asking me out on a date?"

"Girl, dinner at my house and a movie ain't any date."

"Oh…" My heart sank.

"Unique, are you still there?"

My little feelings got hurt and I had to get off the phone. "I'm still here. Look, I have a lot of homework to do. I'll get back to you about dinner and the movie."

"Unique, wait girl, I was just kidding. Can't you take a joke?"

"Ha, ha, very funny, Grant." In an instance I was smiling so hard my cheeks started to hurt and that tingling sensation was back.

"Unique, what are you thinking about?"

"Nothing, I'm not thinking about nothing."

"Tell the truth girl, you were thinking about our kiss, weren't you?"

I couldn't believe I started to blush. "No, I wasn't. I told you I'm doing my homework."

Grant was chuckling. "Okay, then Miss Unique, you go back to your Spanish."

"Adios, Grant."

"Unique."

"Yeah?"

"I got plenty more of those kisses."

"Bye, Grant." I said as I quickly slammed the phone in his ear.

"Dag…that girl is tripping. Maybe, just maybe I will be able to get to third base."

Oh, my…more kisses. On that note, I threw my Spanish book on the floor and turned off the lights. It was time to go to bed. I couldn't fall asleep fast enough because tomorrow, Friday would be here and Grant and I were unofficially having our first date.

Chapter 4

"Unique ! Unique! Get the fuck up out of bed! Didn't you hear the alarm clock? It has been ringing for damn near twenty minutes."

Oh my goodness, the dream I had about Grant lasted all night. This was a first, I never over-sleep. But I know one thing Daddy's foul mood was not going to spoil my day. No way, no how.

I yelled back, "Sorry, Daddy."

"Sorry, hell. You are going to miss the damn bus. Hurry up! I'll take your ass to school. Just don't make this a habit."

"Thanks Daddy." I responded as I bounced past and kissed him on the cheek, he looked at me like I had just lost my mind. I have lost it. My mind was completely cluttered with thoughts of Grant.

On the way to school, I asked Daddy if I could go to dinner later in the evening and to the movies. For once, he didn't give me a hard time about going. Well... I really didn't tell him it was at Grant's house because he automatically assumed I would be with Char or Ruby. I definitely was not going to tell him anything to the contrary because if he found out I was with Grant I would probably end up in a grave next to my mother.

I thought Daddy had a girlfriend because when he decided to come home he was so worn out. Daddy showered and went straight to bed. He barely spoke to me, which was a good thing. I needed a break from his verbal abuse.

I wished he would let me change schools but that damn jailhouse of a school went all the way up to the twelfth grade. I was in prison until then.

The school day dragged on for what seemed like an eternity. I couldn't concentrate at all. Lord knew what I got on my Spanish test. To top it off, I had a surprise Algebra test. Ugh...I hated to see that grade.

I ran all the way home from the bus stop. I just wanted to get home, take a bath, and find the perfect dress to wear. I was extremely excited. I wanted to make a good and lasting impression on Grant's parents.

While soaking in the tub, I thought about how I needed to spend more time with Grant. Even though we didn't attend the same school I wanted everyone to know I was Grant's girl. I guess I'm jumping ahead of myself. It was only one kiss and he probably kissed a lot of girls since then.

I was so thrilled basketball season was about to begin, that would give me plenty of chances to see Grant in action. Since Char and Ruby was on the cheerleading squad, I used them as an excuse to go to the games.

It was funny to me how Daddy never seemed to question me as to where I was going as long as I told him I was with either Char or Ruby. Little did Daddy know Char and Ruby were no longer little girls but young women who got sex on a regular basis. It had been six months since my fourteenth birthday and everything down there was still intact. I had no desire to get my cherry busted, at least not now. However, I wouldn't mind exploring and expanding the sensation I felt with Grant. My body seemed to quiver every time I thought about it.

Oh…my, it was almost six o'clock and I was supposed to be at Grant's house in fifteen minutes but I still haven't found anything to wear. I would wear my favorite dark green turtleneck with the suede dark green checkered and beige skirt. I would top it off with green tights and patent leather black shoes. I was not trying to be revealing, like I really have something to reveal. What a joke. I was barley in a "C" cup.

I still had a bottle of Mother's best perfume. I sprayed a little on me, grabbed my coat, and up the street I went. I arrived at the Johnson's house in three minutes. That was a record. The crisp breeze made the night air very chilly. It was about thirty five degrees outside but I was so hot with excitement and anticipation I thought I would explode! I rang the doorbell and paced back and forth on the front porch. It seemed to take forever before someone answered the door. I heard a woman's voice yelling from behind the closed door.

"Grant! Grant!"

"Yes Mom?"

"Can't you hear the doorbell ringing? Get it. I'm changing your sister."

"Sorry, Mom, I was blasting my radio."

I started to shake to death, not because it was cold but because I thought I would faint when he opened the door.

"Hi, Unique."

"Hi, Grant."

From some room upstairs I heard a woman yell. "Grant, is that your friend Unique at the door?"

"Yes Momma. It's her."

"Great. You two go into the family room. I'll be right down."

"Okay, Momma."

"Give her something to drink. Show her you got manners."

"Dag…Momma."

"Excuse me?"

"Yes Mom."

I laughed at the serious look Grant had on his face but I changed my mind. I didn't want to spoil our evening.

"Come on, girl." Grant said as we walked the winding corridor to the back of the house where the family room was situated.

"Grant, your house is beautiful. You all must be rich?"

"No. I'm not rich. As my Daddy says over and over again, he and momma got money. I have nothing."

"Oh." I said as continued to survey the house.

I was in awe of the superbly decorated home which was painted with such rich exquisite colors which I had never seen before. There were lots of plants in every room as well as limited edition paintings by African American artists which adorned the walls of the Johnson home. Other African American artifacts were strategically placed throughout the house. Each room of the house was more breathtaking than the last.

We walked into the family room where the boys were glued to the television watching Sesame Street.

Grant grabbed the remote control from the black coffee table and changed the channel to What's Happening. Immediately, the boys started to cry.

"Grant, what have you done to your brothers?" Mrs. Johnson asked as she approached the family room.

"Mom, honestly I didn't do anything to them. I just turned off that stupid show."

Mrs. Johnson continued to stroll gracefully toward us. "Here, take your sister. You must be Unique. It is so nice to finally meet you. Grant speaks so highly of you. Unique, you are much prettier than he described." Mrs. Johnson reached for my hand as I responded to her kindness.

Mrs. Johnson wore a pair of red leather pants with a matching red cardigan sweater with white stripes. Every time I saw Mrs.

Johnson zooming past me in her car or walking into her house, she always wore something red. I gathered red must be her favorite color.

Mrs. Johnson was a very regal looking, graceful, and elegant woman who always walked with her head held up high. Her keen dark features made her rare with beauty. Now I saw where Grant got his beautiful eyes. I was truly nervous and didn't want to say anything which would make me seem stupid.

"It's nice to meet you too, Mrs. Johnson. Your house is beautiful. It looks like something out of Jet Magazine or a movie. When I grow up, I want to have a house just like this."

Mrs. Johnson patted me on the back. "Well honey, I'm sure your Momma has your house fixed up real nice too. I need to walk down the street and meet her someday since it looks like you and my Grant will be seeing a lot of each other. Maybe you're momma and I can go to the mall and shop until we drop. Your momma does like to shop, doesn't she? "

Grant shot a crazy look at his mother.

Mrs. Johnson's demeanor changed as she began to chastise Grant. "Boy, why are you looking at me like you have lost your mind? I don't want to discipline you in front of your company but you know I will."

I don't know why I felt like I was cut off guard with the question. I knew it would be a topic of discussion sooner or later. I focused my attention toward the television. A commercial break had just ended as What's Happening retuned and overweight Rerun had just entered Raj's house. Out of the corner of my eye I see Grant giving his mother a weird look.

"Momma…um…Unique's mother is dead."

The pregnant pause was deafening. "Oh, honey, I'm so sorry." Mrs. Johnson grabbed me and gave me a hug. She almost smothered me with her big breasts.

Mrs. Johnson spoke to me with such affection. "If there is anything you ever need to talk about and don't feel like talking to your Daddy, you know, like about girl stuff I'm always available. Any time my poor dear, any time, day or night. I mean it."

"Thank you, Mrs. Johnson." I whispered as I tried to pull away from her suffocating embrace.

Like magic, a giant looking, robust man entered the oversized family room. The triplets screamed "Daddy! Daddy! Daddy!" as they ran into his knees.

I had to strain my neck as I looked up to Mr. Johnson. "Wow...Grant, your Daddy sure is tall."

Grant chuckled. "Yeah, he's six-eight. Thank goodness, I got his height. I would have never gotten into basketball being as short as Momma."

"Yeah, you're right about that. Your mom looks so small next to him and the babies look like midgets."

We both started rolling with laughter.

Mrs. Johnson interrupted our private joke. "Grant, where are your manners? Introduce your friend to your Daddy."

Grant politely shoved me toward his father. "Daddy, this is Unique."

Mr. Johnson grabbed my hand to shake it. I watched in amazement as my hand actually disappeared in his. I could only imagine what Grant went through when his daddy was kicking his butt.

"Nice to meet you honey. She's a cute little thing, isn't she Ingrid?"

I stood there blushing in awe of the tall, bulky man who seemed larger than life. His deep voice reminded me of Barry White.

Mrs. Johnson let out a slight laugh. She gave Mr. Johnson a quick peck on the lips and then she proceeded to the kitchen. "Dinner's ready. Grant, please help me put the kids in their high chairs."

I thought now would be a good time as ever to make brownie points with Mrs. Johnson. I politely followed her and Grant into the kitchen. Then I put on my best smiling face asking, "Is there anything I can do to help you, Mrs. Johnson? I can fold the napkins or help take the food out to the table."

"Oh honey, you are just so thoughtful, but no, just sit down right there, next to Mr. Johnson and make your self comfortable."

I was very apprehensive about sitting next to Mr. Johnson. I barely knew the man but something about him made me feel so uncomfortable. I guess I was just being paranoid.

As everyone got settled in his or her seats at the dining room table, Mr. Johnson reached for my hand. On his right side, he grabbed Mrs. Johnson's hand. Grant nudged me to hold his hand.

Mr. Johnson cleared his throat and bowed his head as he spoke. I thought we were about to have a Sunday sermon. "Heavenly Father, we thank you for the food that we are about to receive and we ask that you bless it in Jesus' name. Amen, amen. Now, everyone dig in. Ingrid, it looks like you outdid yourself tonight. Yes, Lord…"

With the blessing of the food, we all began to dig in. Grant's family made me a bit envious. My family never ate together, let alone did anyone say a blessing. So this is what a normal family does? Boy, have I been missing out. "Oh well…" I muttered under my breath, as I looked at all the food that was on the table.

Grant's mother really prepared a spread of food. There was macaroni and cheese, fried pork chops smothered in gravy, candied sweet potatoes, and collard greens mixed with kale. The peach cobbler she baked in the oven engulfed the entire house with its sweet aroma. It smelled so good I just wanted to skip dinner and head straight for the dessert.

Mr. Johnson told Mrs. Johnson about his hectic day. How he had a big murder case he was hearing. I gathered Mr. Johnson was a judge or an attorney. I couldn't figure out exactly what Mrs. Johnson did but I knew she worked at a bank downtown.

The triplets were making a mess as they unsuccessfully attempted to feed themselves.

I sat next to Grant and underneath the table he kept sliding his hand up my skirt while I tried not to wiggle and get caught. I had to shove food in my mouth to keep from screaming every time I felt the rush Grant was giving me as he touched and rubbed my thighs. When he touched the edge of my panties, I almost jumped out of my seat. Thank the Lord; the Johnsons were absorbed in their conversation. I shot Grant the dirtiest look I could muster up. Of course, Grant stopped after he winked at me and gave me a sheepish grin which was plastered on his face.

Abruptly, the Johnsons conversation came to a halt and they directed their attention to me. Beads of perspiration formed on my brow from my little table tryst. I just knew Grant and I were busted. The baritone voice of Mr. Johnson startled me.

"So, Unique, Grant tells me you attend the all-white girls' school down there on Fifth Avenue. Your parents must do well for themselves. Tell me what do they do for a living?"

Oh, boy, here we go again, I thought to myself. People either liked my Daddy or they didn't, there was no in-between.

"Well, sir, my mother died a few years ago."

"Oh, I'm so sorry to hear that my dear child. What a tragedy it must be to lose your mother at your young age. You must miss her guidance terribly."

I just nodded in agreement as Mr. Johnson kept on talking. "Well, your Daddy must have a great job. Because these houses around here cost an arm and a leg and he sends you to a private school. He must be well off. Yes indeed, he must make a pretty penny."

Mrs. Johnson injected herself into the conversation. "Justin, please the girl is not in one of your courts. Why do you always have to interrogate everyone? Besides, whatever her father does for a living really isn't any of our concern."

"Ingrid, I'm not trying to cross-examine the young lady. I'm just trying to find out some family background, that's all. Our son has his nose all-open by this young girl, so I need to know whom he is dealing with. Now, you wouldn't want him to be so strung out on a girl who's Daddy might be involved in some sort of illegal activity. Now would you? Tell the truth now, Ingrid."

Mrs. Johnson huffed and quickly turned her attention toward me. "Unique, darling, I truly apologize for my husband's rather rude behavior. Don't pay Mr. Johnson any attention. He really is a very nice man. He's a teddy bear once you get to know him. Aren't you, darling?"

"It's okay. Mrs. Johnson." I said as I gave a weak smile. My knees were shaking underneath the table. Then Grant put his two cents in.

"Daddy, her father is the mayor of Pittsburgh."

Mr. Johnson's entire demeanor changed right before our very eyes. The man who appeared to be such a loving father and devoted husband was quickly shifting into this life form filled with complete anger and hatred.

I started to tremble from the inside out. I felt I was watching a horror flick unraveling right before my eyes. Chiller Theater had nothing on this. I was in the belly of the beast.

Mr. Johnson cranked his neck toward Grant. "What did you say, boy? Did I hear you correctly? He's the fucking mayor? Are you telling me Morris Blackman is her father?"

Sheepishly, Grant answered, "Yes, Sir."

"I'll be damn. I can't believe I moved up the street from that passing-for-white motherfucker. That no good bastard."

"Justin! Have you lost your mind?" Mrs. Johnson stood up with authority.

The rattling of Mr. Johnson's voice made the triplets cry. I just sat there wobbly in my seat with my head lowered. I was scared to move an inch.

"I'm sorry Grant, but this girl has to leave my house right this instance and don't you ever bring her back here again."

Tears rolled down my face as I methodically moved away from the dining room table.

Grant choked back his tears as he looked at his father in disbelief. "Daddy, what is wrong with you? Why are you being so mean to my friend? How can you be so rude?"

"Grant, get her out of here!" Mr. Johnson said as he slammed his humongous hand down on the dinner table. The table, the glasses, and the silverware shook and moved as a title wave of emotion flooded the room.

Mrs. Johnson looked at Mr. Johnson with horror in her eyes. She was completely thrown by his unexpected outburst.

"Justin! What in the world? Grant…"

"Yes Momma?" Grant said as he tried to find some comfort in his mother's voice.

Mrs. Johnson threw her napkin on the table and frantically pushed back her chair and walked briskly to where Grant and I were sitting. She motioned for us to get up and hastily walked us toward the door.

We arrived at the front door and Mrs. Johnson's extended her delicate hands and cupped my chin as she spoke. "My precious Unique, I am so embarrassed. I am sorry about this. Here is your coat. Grant, walk Unique home and get back here right away."

"Yes Momma," Grant said as tears filled his eyes. He helped me with my coat and turned to his mother.

"Momma what is wrong? Why is Daddy acting like this? How could he do this to me?"

"Go ahead honey. Take Unique home. We will talk when you get back. Now go." Mrs. Johnson said as she kissed Grant gently on his forehead.

Grant held my hand tightly as we walked down the street. Tears poured out of my eyes like water flowing effortlessly from a broken pipe.

My voice was barely audible as I spoke, "Grant, my father is not me. Why does your father hate my dad so much?"

"I don't know, Unique. I had no idea my dad even knew your father. You have to calm down. Getting hysterical won't change the situation. Listen to me, Unique; whatever difficulty my dad has with your father is his problem. I still want to see you."

"How can we see each other when your dad hates me?"

"Look at me, Unique."

"I can't. I feel so bad."

Grant stopped halfway to my house and grabbed my face. I looked into his swollen eyes Grant spoke to me with such tenderness, "Unique Blackman, I promise you we will still continue to see each other. One day you're going to be my wife. You have to trust me." Grant gave me a quick kiss on the cheek and in a flash he ran back home to the sounds of his fighting parents.

Chapter 5

"Justin Ellington Johnson, what in the hell just happened here? I can't believe you acted like a damn fool. No, you weren't a fool you were really a complete ass. I can't understand how you could embarrass your son and this family like that."

"I'm sorry Ingrid, but you know I can't stand that bastard. I've hated him ever since college. Morris Blackman has always been a thorn in my side. He's been a festering, puss-infected sore that has never gone away!"

"Yes dear, I know the entire scenario. There is no need for you to rehash your story. If I've heard it once I've heard it a thousand times. But you need to grow up. It's been along time since your college days. Besides you can't blame the sins of the father on the daughter. She has nothing to do with this. Your son's feelings are at stake here. Grant's feelings should come first. He really likes Unique. I think he is in love."

"Ingrid, he's in love? That boy doesn't know the first thing about being in love. He will be in love a dozen times before he marries. All I know at this moment is our son will have to get over Unique Blackman. I refuse to let that son of a bitch ruin my son's life."

"My God, Justin, do you hear yourself? You are just going too far with this rivalry thing. How can you change what our son is feeling in his heart? Justin, Grant is not a faucet; you can't turn his feelings off or on. Honey, our son is not in one of your courts you can't control this part of his life."

"Ingrid, I don't know how I will change Grant's feelings but I will. Even if I have to die trying, this relationship for him is over! You think this has something to do with a rivalry with Morris Blackman? No, it's more than that. He has blocked every position I have ever tried to obtain. He tries to sabotage me every opportunity that he gets. Besides that, you know he killed my Jenny."

"What the hell did you just say?"

"Unique's mother, Jenny, was my girlfriend in college. This happened way before you went to Spelman."

"What? Why is this the first time I am hearing about Jenny? I've heard your war stories with Morris but you have failed to mention Jenny in the past. What other secrets are you hiding from me?"

"Ingrid, please let me finish. When we were pledging, Morris treated me the worst. He treated me like I was an illegal alien trying to sneak into the country. That man always talked about my color. Morris said that I wasn't light enough or handsome enough to be a Kappa. He said the color of my skin remind him of the shit he would flush down the toilet. Morris gave me my line name, Little Brother Shit A Lot. Can you believe that? The brothers thought it was funny as hell. He did everything he could do to break me, but I held on. I crossed the burning sands. Morris was outraged when I became his frat."

"I'm confused Justin. I still don't understand what that has got to do with Unique's mother and why you never mentioned this to me before."

"Ingrid, some things you should just leave alone. Everything else you know. When you arrived at Spelman, Jenny and I had been broken up for at least a year."

"So what does this have to do with Morris?"

"Ingrid, stop pacing back and fourth. Sit down, Ingrid."

"No! I'd rather stand."

"Have it your way. Like I was saying Ingrid, Jenny was my girlfriend. When Jenny was younger, she used to have a crush on Morris but he ignored her. But things changed when she went to college and started going out with me. Morris knew how much Jenny meant to me but he just didn't give a damn. He saw Jenny as a trophy, another way for him to stab me in the back. Morris started paying Jenny lots of attention by sending her flowers and things. He finally won her over. It broke my heart but it was to be expected from that mother fucker. He always had it in for me and still does."

"Justin apparently Jenny wasn't into you as you thought if she could leave you over some damn flowers. As I see it, you two really didn't have much of a relationship if it was so easy for another man to woo her away."

"Well Ingrid, we were together and very close. I guess you had to be there!"

"I guess so! Justin, aren't you being presumptuous in accusing Morris of killing his wife? How do you know he killed her? What evidence do you have? That's a huge allegation to make against anyone. I've never read anything in the newspapers to confirm your suspicions. There was never any formal investigation."

"You're right, Ingrid. There was never any investigation. Everything Morris Blackman does is always done in the dark. Jenny used to call me at work."

"Wait a minute! What the hell was she doing calling you? And how long had this been going on? Justin, I see you had another life I apparently knew nothing about!"

"Ingrid, it wasn't about having another life. We always kept in touch. I just never told you. I didn't think you would be happy with me talking to my ex-girlfriend all of the time. Jenny would tell me how Morris would beat her. I tried to convince her to leave. I offered to get her and the child into a safe house but she was too afraid. She said it would be dangerous for me to get involved."

"Justin, you're damn right I would be mad at you. And I am mad at you. After all the years we have been together, you didn't give me the common courtesy to tell me any of this. If you had given me a chance, I would have understood if you explained everything to me. Maybe I could have helped. Right now, I'm stunned and pissed at you! How could you keep this from me? Justin, please tell me the truth, I need to know, where you sleeping with her?"

"No…Ingrid! Absolutely not! For Christ sake, I would never cheat on you. You've got to believe me. You and the kids are my heart and soul, my life. Jenny knew that too. She just needed a friend, that's all. The day before Jenny died she called me and said she had enough of Morris's abuse. She was finally ready to go to the safe house. Jenny said she had a doctor's appointment because she was miserable with chronic headaches. She agreed to meet me after work. But she never came. The following morning I read in the paper she had died."

"Justin, I don't know if I should feel sorry you lost a friend. What I feel like is slapping the hell out of you for keeping secrets from me. But the actions you displayed tonight in front of our son and his guess were inexcusable!"

"Ingrid, I haven't lost you, have I?"

"No…dear. But tonight you can sleep on the couch!"

"I … I know I shouldn't have kept this from you. I… I just didn't want you to take it the wrong way. I didn't think you would understand Jenny and I remained friends over the years. I can't believe I live a few doors away from that murderer."

"I always knew you hated Morris because of your college days. I assumed the hate continued when he wouldn't endorse you as City Councilman. Morris then continued to snub you when you were appointed to the judges' bench. I see now it was more than that… all along it was about you still having feelings for Jenny."

"Well…Ingrid all I can say is Jenny was just a small part of the picture. Honestly, Ingrid, please believe me. I have always been too black, too inferior for the high standards of the righteous high yellow, Morris Blackman the third."

"Ingrid, where's Grant? I need to apologize to him. I hope somehow I can make things right between us."

"I don't know where he is, Justin. He should have been home a while ago. Don't think you can make Grant forgive you so quickly. The hurt I saw in our son's eyes is very deep. I've never seen him look so… distraught…so devastated."

"I know, Ingrid. I saw the look too. I guess I have messed up everything. I'll be back. I'm going to look for him."

Mr. Johnson put on his coat and opened the door. There sat Grant on the front porch. Grant had been crying and was now frozen from being out in the cold so long. Mr. Johnson gently placed his hand on Grant's shoulder.

"Son, I was getting ready to look for you. Come in the house before you catch a cold. We need to talk about some things. How about I fix you some hot chocolate, with marshmallows on top?"

Grant brushed his father's hand away from his shoulder and yelled. "I don't want to talk to you! I don't want anything from you! I hate you!"

In one swift move Mr. Johnson snatched Grant up by his coat collar, lifting him in the air so they could be face to face. Mr. Johnson's breath was hot and spit spewed from his mouth as he spoke: "Boy, as long as you live don't you ever tell me that again or I will wear your narrow behind out. Do you understand me?"

Grant could only nod as he looked down at his feet dangling in the air.

Mr. Johnson let his venom out once more. "Now, get your ass in the house."

Mr. Johnson lowered Grant and popped him upside his head so hard Grant's neck wobbled from side to side.

Mr. Johnson huffed. "Consider that a warning, young man. You must have forgotten whom you were speaking to. I can see that girl has already put her hooks into you."

Through his sobs Grant spoke. "Daddy, you were so mean to Unique. I love her!"

"Grant, you will love a whole bunch of girls in your lifetime before you settle down and find your wife. You have to believe me on that one, son."

"You're wrong, Daddy! You don't know a thing about Unique. I did find my wife. I'm going to marry her! You just wait and see! There is nothing you can do about it."

"Grant Montgomery Johnson, if you want to live in this house under my roof, then I forbid you to see that girl! Her family is bad news. You hear me, boy! Leave her alone!"

Grant stomped down the hall and shouted "I hate you." as he slammed his bedroom door.

"Boy, I'll kill you! Got damn it where is my belt? I'm going to tear that boy a new asshole. Who in the hell does he think he is? You're nothing but a disrespectful punk!"

"Justin, just stop it! Please leave him alone! You are not going to take your anger out on our son! You've caused enough damage for tonight. Goodnight." Mrs. Johnson said as she threw two pillows and blanket at Mr. Johnson hitting him in the head.

"But…Ingrid. We need to talk."

"Justin, I don't need to talk to you anymore tonight! I have a headache and I'm going to bed by myself! Enjoy the couch."

"But…"

Mrs. Johnson slammed her bedroom door and locked it leaving a frustrated Justin behind.

Chapter 6

Winter turned to spring, spring turned to summer, and summer turned to fall. Before we knew it, Grant and I were in our senior year of high school. We were both anticipating the prom, graduation, college, and our life together.

As all of the years passed by, Grant and I continued to sneak to see each other. With friends like Char and Ruby covering for me, it wasn't hard to find time to spend with Grant. Most of the time we spent together was at my house since my Daddy hardly came home. Grant and I actually had a nice little set up so we thought.

Prom time was approaching fast. I had decided not to go to my prom. Who would want to go to a prom with a bunch of white girls and their dates? Not me. I told Daddy I'd rather spend my time at Char and Ruby's prom. Daddy didn't object. I was on cloud nine. Grant and I would have a wonderful time together.

Daddy didn't make a big deal about the prom because he was busy preparing his commencement speech for my graduation. I was so upset when Principal Greer called me into his office to tell me the good news. He thought Daddy speaking at graduation was good timing, considering Daddy was also about to run for Governor of the State of Pennsylvania. Principal Greer was one of Daddy's supporters.

Daddy rarely had time for me. He only needed me when the press wanted to do a photo session of the Blackman's happy family. If the press only knew, exactly what went on behind our closed doors they would be totally shocked. My father would definitely be knocked off of his high pedestal.

For years, Mrs. Johnson kept the secret Grant and I were seeing each other. When she looked in her son's eyes she could see the love he had for me. Mrs. Johnson even took me shopping to for my prom dress. I loved her so much. She was like a mother to me.

Prom night was simply magical. Grant looked handsome in his black tux accented with a pink carnation in his lapel. Mr. Johnson was very displeased I was Grant's date but he went and rented us a chaffered driven limousine. Mrs. Johnson had to pull out some new tricks in the bedroom in order to get Mr. Johnson out of his evil mood.

I was pretty in pink in a low cut spaghetti strapped gown that crisscrossed in the back. This was the first time I was showing some cleavage and I loved it. The gown hugged me in all the right places. The frock was so form-fitting I could barely move. I was almost walking like Morticia from the Adams Family as I floated my way to the limousine.

This was one of the most important days of my life and my Dad was out of town. He was missing one of the biggest events of my senior year. To Daddy, my special event was just another day for him. I felt alone. There was no one at my house to cry with, to be excited with, or to take pictures of my special day. I really missed my Mother. My soul ached to for one of her hugs. She gave me the best hugs. I wanted so much to see Mother's smile as I twirled around again and again in my dress. I wanted to her say how beautiful I was as she planted kisses all over my face while snapping a bunch of Polaroids. We would have had so much fun together doing all the girly things us girls do to get ready for a big event.

Instead, my girls Char and Ruby made a fuss over me. They tried so hard to fill my void. They even took me to get my hair and nails done. They meant well but it just wasn't the same as having your mother around.

The limo picked us up at Char's house. Their dates were already there. Char wore a beautiful asymmetrical navy gown. Her date looked like a big blue peacock. Ruby's date was dashing in a black tux with tails. Ruby, of course, wore a ruby red dress which had a sweetheart neckline and was off the shoulders. The gown had a split which went all the way up her left leg almost exposing her goodies.

But no one could touch Grant! He was absolutely the most handsome boy at the prom. I knew Char and Ruby were jealous but they hid it well.

When Grant saw me in my dress his eyes lit up like fireworks at the Fourth of July. His dazzling smile was devastating. He made me tingle from the top of my head to the bottom of my feet. I felt as if I were in a fairy tale.

"Wow! Unique, you look incredibly beautiful."

"Thank you, Mr. Johnson. You don't look so bad yourself."

Mrs. Johnson dragged Mr. Johnson and the triplets over Char's house to take pictures. She was gushing with pride.

"Look at them Justin. Aren't they just adorable?" Mrs. Johnson said as the camera clicked away. I swear we took at least a hundred photos before Mrs. Johnson would let us go. I thought we would miss the prom.

Grant checked his watch. "Mom, please it's getting late we need to get going."

"Okay, Grant." Mrs. Johnson said as she wiped a tear from her eye.

Grant put his arm around his mother and gave her a good hug. "Come on, Momma. You're embarrassing me. Why are you crying?"

"Oh, go ahead boy. You just look so handsome. You remind me of your father on our wedding day. Have fun, be home before two or you'll turn into a pumpkin and I'll have to send your father looking for you."

"Mom, are you really serious? Two?"

"Yes, indeed. I mean two. If you keep yapping your mouth, it will be one."

I quickly grabbed Grant. "Come on, Grant. Let's go before you ruin everything."

Our evening was magical. Grant and I were starring in our own motion picture. Nothing else and no one else mattered in or world. It was just Grant and I tangled up in our love. We danced and danced all night long. Love songs played from A Love of Your Own by the Average White Band to the last song of the night, The Reasons by Earth, Wind, and Fire.

Grant was grinding and holding on to me so hard I thought he was about to have an orgasm right there on the dance floor.

"Damn...Unique, you feel so good and smell so...wonderful. Did you know you are the prettiest girl at this prom? All my boys are upset because their girls don't even come close to looking as good as you."

"I am not the prettiest girl here, but thank you."

"Yes, you are! Trust and believe. All my homeboys are mad jealous. They said I was wrong for hiding you. Now they all want to visit your school to see if they can find them a beautiful girl. I tried to tell them you are one of a kind."

"That's right I'm Unique and don't you forget it."

We looked into each other's eyes and passionately kissed on the dance floor. Both of us knew tonight would be the night I would give him my virginity. Grant had patiently waited four long years. Besides, I was the last of my friends to get my cherry busted. Char and Ruby gave me all kinds of condoms and instructions on what to expect. They even took me to get my first pack of birth control pills.

Prom night was over but it was just a new beginning for us. The limo dropped off all of the kids and we made it home way before our curfew. I got out of the limo and rushed into the empty house. I quickly took my shower and waited for Grant to sneak out of his house so we could make love for the very first time.

I had fallen asleep when I heard a knock at the front door. I was a little afraid because it was now five in the morning. I looked in the peephole and there he was my Grant, my night in shining armor.

Sleepily, I asked Grant, "What took you so long?"

"Unique, do I really need to answer that? You know my mom; she was up waiting for me. She wanted every detail. I never thought she would go to sleep. I have to be home before six thirty, that's when Pops gets up."

"Grant, that doesn't give us much time."

"I know. I'm sorry but I promise to make it up to you. Are you sure your pops isn't going to roll in here?"

"He left me a message; he's in Michigan and won't be back until tomorrow evening."

"Well, Miss Blackman let's get this party started."

I giggled as Grant swopped me off of my feet and took me upstairs to my bedroom.

I was a nervous wreck. I started to perspire profusely as I watched Grant undress. His muscular chest was a spectacular masterpiece accentuated with defined chiseled ripples which flowed downward to the beginning of his pubic hairs. He unleashed his member which seemed to have a life of its own as it slithered like a snake out of his underwear. It was wide, long and hard. Exposed and ready to enter me for the very first time. How in the world was that going to fit in me? Seeing a penis up close and personal was indescribable. I suppose what I viewed was indeed splendid but what did I know?

I lay on the bed as my insides shook. Grant undressed me with each kiss he planted so tenderly on my body. Before I knew it, our bodies were in a unified dance, entangled, and entwined in a rhythmical melody all its own. Gentle moans escaped into the early morning, as time kept moving, leaving us unaware the clock was turning to seven. Our encounter left me dazed with an indescribable feeling of euphoria. Sweat rolled off of me and soaked the once pristine sheets. I wiped the damp hair from my face and turned toward the red illumination of the clock which was on my nightstand across from my bed.

Horror struck me as I looked at the digital display and shouted, "Grant!"

Barley moving, Grant rolled over and kissed my shoulder. "What Unique? Damn. Can't you wake a brother up more peacefully?"

I pushed Grant off of my shoulder. "Grant, look at the time! Your father is going to kill us!"

Nonchalantly, Grant sat up in the bed. "Calm down, Unique. I've got it covered. You know my bedroom is in the back of the house on the first floor. I took the screen out and left the window open. I had counted on your good loving to last longer than expected."

With a sigh of relief I gently nudged Grant. "Grant, do you know how crazy you are?"

Grant jumped up from the bed and threw on his jeans and oversized Steelers sweatshirt. "I am crazy and hopelessly in love with you. Catch you later and lock the door."

We kissed goodbye. I watched Grant until he disappeared toward the back of his house.

I locked the front door and proceeded to take a shower. My emotional state was in turmoil. Our lovemaking had left me feeling a bit dirty and ecstatic all at the same time. I was forever changed, forever in love.

Chapter 7

As graduation day approached, I started feeling sick. It usually was in the morning but sometimes it lasted awhile.

Grant had applied to all the top rated colleges. He was so excited when he got the news he received a full scholarship to play basketball in California at Stanford University. I was extremely happy for him. He was about to embark in the greatest adventure of his lifetime. Grant was a step closer in fulfilling his dream of one day, playing professional basketball. He was very enthused about this new chapter of his life but I knew our life would never be like it used to be. Grant swore to me he wouldn't date anyone else and he would work and save his money so he could fly me out to California to visit.

Char, Ruby, and I were going to Spelman. Spelman was Mrs. Johnson's and my Mom's alma mater. Mrs. Johnson was so happy for me. Little did I know a change was coming and it was going to come extremely fast, faster than I expected.

"Hello…Char?"

"This is Char. Is this Unique? What's up girl…? You sound like you were crying. Hold on while I call Ruby. We can have a three way."

"Okay." I said solemnly.

"Ruby…?"

"Yeah, this is Ruby."

"This is Char. I have Unique on the other line something's wrong. She's been crying."

"What is it, Unique?" My two best friends screamed at me all at once.

"I…I…I… think I'm pregnant."

"Pregnant?" They both shrieked at me again.

"Girl, didn't you take those pills we gave you?" Ruby said in a concerned voice.

"We told you to use condoms too." Alarmed, Char shouted at me.

"Well…actually I kept forgetting to take the pills and that night happened so fast we forgot to use the condoms."

"Unique, we drilled it in your head for you to take those pills everyday." Char advised me rudely.

"I know but..."

"Stop crying, Unique. Do you know for sure? Have you told Grant?" asked Ruby.

"No, I haven't said anything to him. I wanted to be positively sure."

"Look, we'll be right over and we will take you to Family Planning. They offer a free clinic. Char, I'm on my way to pick you up."

"Okay, Ruby, I'll be ready."

Char tried to sound sympathetic. "Unique, you need to stop crying until we find out for sure."

"Thanks you two. I'll see you in a bit."

The stark white walls of the free clinic were filled with pictures of pregnant women in different stages of pregnancy. The pictures of the babies seemed to jump out at you. The office was filled with young girls and older women, some who were pregnant and some were anxiously waiting to find out if motherhood was in their foreseeable future. When we walked into the clinic, it seemed as though everyone was diverting their attention toward us. I guess paranoia had set in.

Off to the left side of the waiting area was registration. A big sign hung above the registration window which read "Sign In." Behind the glass window sat a receptionist who looked like she was barely old enough to work in such a place.

I was about to sign in when the young woman spoke, "May I help you?"

"Uh…uh…um…um…I'm here…to take a-a-a-pregnancy test."

The receptionist looked at me like I was retarded. I was feeling uncomfortable about the entire situation. She looked at me like she was disturbed by my presence. She pushed a piece of hair away from her eye before she spoke.

"After you sign in take this cup to the bathroom down the hall on the left hand side and put a urine sample in it. You can leave the cup in the little silver door over the sink. Someone will call you when the results are ready."

"Thank you." I said sheepishly.

"Wait a minute." The receptionist hollered at me.

"Yes…?" I said not looking into her eyes.

"You need to fill out this questionnaire. Here's a pen. Please complete all of the forms and return it to me when you are finished. If you have an insurance card I'll make a copy of it too."

"Okay." I walked toward Ruby and Char. Both of them were looking at me full of anticipation.

Ruby spoke first. "Well, what do you have to do now?"

"I have to fill out this paperwork, piss in this cup, and then they will call me with the results."

"How long will it take?" Asked a nervous, Char.

"I don't know. I didn't think to ask. Hold my coat. I'll be back in a moment."

I headed toward the ladies room. Each step I took seemed to take longer than the first. My feet felt as if they were made of lead sinking fast in a puddle of quick sand as they were unwilling to lift one at a time.

I couldn't urinate at first. I just sat there on the cold porcelain toilet for about fifteen minutes and cried. Finally, I got up and turned on some water and bingo, a rush of urine flew out.

My hands shook as I placed the plastic container in the little door above the sink. Well it was done. I would soon know my fate. I washed my hands and walked out of the restroom to a line of angry women waiting to use the facilities.

As I approached Ruby she yelled, "It's about time you came out of there."

Char pointed her finger in my direction. "Yeah, girl, I thought I was going to have come and pull you off of the toilet. Are you okay?"

"No, Char, I'm not okay. I don't know if I'll ever be okay again."

Ruby, Char, and I held each other's hands as we anticipated my results. We quietly sat in the waiting room, shaking. Time stood still as we waited another twenty-five minutes.

Finally, an old, gray-haired nurse came out and scanned the room full of women. She looked at her chart and said, "Miss Unique Blackman." All three of us stood. The nurse waved for us to follow her. She led us to a small conference room and pointed for us to take a seat.

"Which one of you is Miss Blackman?" said the nurse as she blew her nose.

"I am Miss Blackman." I said as I shook in my shoes. Char and Ruby were on either side of me still holding my hands for support.

"I must advise you Miss Blackman these results are confidential. Do you still want your friends to be in here?"

"Yes, I want them to stay," I said in a quivering voice.

"Well then Miss Blackman, I have your results. Today is your lucky day. Congratulations! You're about three months pregnant. Go to the front desk and schedule another appointment for an internal exam. You should schedule the exam within the next few days. I have some brochures for you regarding the birthing process, adoption, and even abortion. Should you choose to go that route, you will need someone to drive you home. Here is a prescription for some prenatal vitamins. You need to start taking them right away and take them once a day preferably with food or a glass of milk. They tend to make some women vomit. Congratulations again. See you in a couple of days."

I was oblivious to the nurse's entire conversation. I felt as if a thick fog surrounded me. I almost fainted but my girls had my back. They escorted me to the car as I wailed like a baby.

"Char, Ruby, what am I going to tell Grant? He's ready to leave for Stanford. My God, between his dad and mine we're are going to get killed."

"Look, Unique. You don't have to have the baby because there are options." Char said looking at me like I knew what she was talking about.

Ruby agreed with Char. "Yeah, Unique, you can give the baby up for adoption."

"Ruby, I wasn't talking about any adoption. I was talking about an abortion."

"An abortion, are you serious?" Ruby and I said in horrified voices.

"Yes, an abortion. There is nothing wrong with your hearing. It's really not as bad as you may think."

"How do you know?" Ruby and I said together.

"Well…I…just know."

"Come on, Char give up the goods." Ruby said looking intently in Char's eyes. While I sat in the back seat and cried like there was no tomorrow. "We never keep secrets from each other."

"Well…I've had three."

"Three!" We shouted at Char.

"When, where, how?" I asked in between my sobs.

"That's not important, Unique, but you can have it done and no one has to know. You're old enough now to sign your consent. Trust me. I wouldn't lie to you. It's as easy as one, two, and three."

"Char, I'm carrying a life, life Grant and I created out of love which is a gift from God. Who knows what my baby might look like; she could look like my Mother. I just couldn't imagine flushing her down the Alleghany River. No, I don't think so."

Ruby nodded her head in agreement. "I'm with you on this one, Unique. A baby is a gift sent straight from heaven."

"You two can believe in the fairy tale shit if you want too. Who's going to buy the babies diapers, formula, and clothes? Who is going take the baby to the doctors when it gets sick? Who's going to buy the baby's diapers and clothes? Unique, do you honestly expect Grant to give up his basketball dreams just for you? Girl, you need to get your head out of the sand and come back to a reality. I hadn't realized you are truly sprung."

"You are wrong, Char. Grant loves me. We were together for four years before I even gave him any."

"That's bull, Unique. I know you've been screwing around as long as me and Ruby."

"I have not!" I said adamantly.

"Char, Unique is telling us the truth. I had to tell her how to give a blow job."

"I swear Ruby, do you tell everything?"

"For real, Unique? You didn't even know how to perform oral sex on your man? Damn, that's deep."

I just shook my head in agreement. There was nothing really to discuss.

We drove the rest of the way home in silence, while I tried to figure out how I was going to tell Grant.

Chapter 8

It took me an entire week to get enough courage to tell Grant he was going to be a daddy. I decided to call Grant and ask him to come down to my house. Usually, we just met outside on my front porch around noon. But today was an exception. It was around nine.

I was a nervous wreck, when Grant knocked on the door. My voice trembled as I asked, "Who is it?"

"It's the love of your life. Come on, Unique, open up."

"Okay," I said with more apprehension as I unlocked the door.

"Hey, gorgeous, how are you this beautiful morning?" Grant said as he planted a juicy kiss on my lips.

For the first time I gently pulled away. Grant gave me a puzzled look. "What's up, baby cakes? You seem distant. You still ain't sweatin' me about going away to college, are you? I told you we will be together forever. I knew it when I first laid eyes on you, before I forget; I've got some news for you. But you go first and tell me your big news because you sure don't look happy."

Briefly, I felt my courage draining from my soul. "No, you go first, Grant. My news isn't going anywhere."

"Are you sure?"

"Yeah, I'm sure. Go ahead. Do you want something to drink?"

"Bring me a Coke."

"You want a Coke? So early in the morning, you must have a stomach made out of steel." I laughed as I went into the kitchen to retrieve the soda. When I got back to the living room Grant was sprawled out on the couch like he owned the place. I guess I had been living on my own for a long while. Daddy seemed to only be home twice a week. He claimed he was working on his campaign for the governor's seat and it was taking up all of his time but I knew better.

"Here you go, Grant."

"Thanks, baby cakes."

"So what is this important news?"

"My pops and moms told me last night that Dad has decided to run for Mayor since your father has decided to move onto bigger and brighter things."

"Oh."

"Oh…is that all you have to say? Unique, this is big stuff. My dad is going to be rolling."

I uttered, "That's nice."

Grant took a gulp of his soda and placed the can on the glass coffee table and looked at me. "Girl, what's wrong with you? And don't tell me nothing is wrong. You have been in a trance ever since I came walking threw that door. And you're the one who called this early morning meeting. Look, if you are on your rag or something then I'm going to bounce and let you be moody all by yourself. I've got packing to do."

Grant got up from the couch and I grabbed his hand. "Wait! Grant. I so desperately need to talk to you."

"Unique, are you sick? You are scarring me. What's going on?"

I shouted at him, "I…I…I am pregnant!"

Grant's beautiful chocolate skin turned pale. He sat back down on the couch and put his head in his hands. "Pregnant?" he whispered.

"Yes, Grant. We are going to be parents in about six months. This is our prom night miracle. Grant, please say something. Do you want me to get an abortion or put the baby up for adoption?"

Grant jumped from the couch, picked me up, and twirled me around.

"Stop, Grant! I'm going to throw up." Grant put me down as I made a mad dash to the bathroom and vomited until I couldn't hurl anymore.

Grant stood behind me with a cold washcloth and wiped my face. I couldn't look at him. Grant lifted my face and looked lovingly into my eyes.

"Unique Blackman, you have made me the happiest man in the world!"

"I did? I do?"

"Yes, you do! You better get all those thoughts about abortion and adoption out of your head. That's my seed in your belly and it's staying right here with us. We can get married next weekend."

"Whoa…hold your horses, next weekend?"

"Yes, Unique. I love you with all of my heart and soul. There is no sense in waiting. I was always going to marry you. It's just sooner rather than later. Damn…I am going to be a daddy!"

"Grant, you are moving way too fast. We need to think things through. What about your basketball scholarship? Going to

Stanford has been your dream for years. Besides, your dad is going to kill you. Then he's going to kill me. Your dad hates me!"

"Well, Unique, Daddy dearest will just have to adjust his attitude. If not, it's too damn bad. This is my life, our life. I'm a grown man."

"Grant you're not that grown. You don't own a house, a car, or have a job. You're just eighteen and a half. Grant, you just don't know how nervous I have been lately. I was so worried you would be upset with me."

"Unique, I hate to tell you this but you didn't get pregnant by yourself. How could you doubt my love? How long have you known? I held out four years to get some good booty. And for your information Miss Unique, I do own a car."

"It's a car your daddy pays for. Hell, he even gives you gas money. Try again, Mr. Johnson."

"Yeah, I guess you're right. But who cares about that? You skated around my question so I'll ask it again. How could you doubt my love for you?"

"Grant, I never doubted your love. I doubted you wanted to be a father right now. You have such a bright future ahead of you. I didn't want to spoil it for you. I didn't want you to have any regrets because then you would start hating me."

"Unique, I could never hate you. You are such a big part of my life I can't even find the right words to explain to you how I feel. Having a child with you only makes me love you more. This might sound silly but my heart sings with joy when I look at you."

"Oh...Grant, I love you so very much."

"Well now, you know I love you too. I will love you until my dying day. We have to tell our parents and that's not going to be so easy. Let's go. My mom is off today we might as well tell her first. Mom can break the ice for us with my dad. How do you think your father will react?"

I sighed and shrugged my shoulders as I paused just trying to visualize my irate father. "Grant I'm frightened. I never told you this but my Daddy used to beat my mother. I truly believe after all the abuse my mom took over the years is why she finally died. He has also abused me on more than one occasion."

"My God, Unique, I can't believe you never shared this with me. I don't remember seeing any bruising on your face."

"I know. Daddy made sure he never damaged my face. Didn't you ever notice I wore a lot of long sleeve tops? Now days it's more verbal abuse than physical. I'm sorry, Grant, I hid this from you. I felt ashamed. That's why I never complain when he's not around. I don't have to worry about when the next attack might come. From this day forward, I promise you no more secrets."

"Unique, your father is a jerk! A real man never abuses his wife or his kids. He's just a punk in a man's body. Don't worry...we will tell your father together. I make you a promise right here; right now your father will never ever put his hands on you again. Not while I'm alive and kicking! You can take that to the bank."

"I love you so much, Grant."

"I love you too. Come on. Let's go and tell my mother."

We held hands while we walked up the street. He held me tight and smothered me with kisses while he rubbed my belly. He was very happy about the baby. We found Mrs. Johnson folding laundry in the family room.

"Hey Mom, are you busy?"

"Hello, Mrs. Johnson."

"Hello you two, Grant, I was wondering where you disappeared to so early in the morning. Did you eat breakfast? Sit down and I'll whip up some waffles and cook some bacon. How does that sound?"

"I'm not hungry, Mrs. Johnson, but thank you."

"Unique, you need to eat, especially now. Go ahead Mom. We both will have something to eat."

"All right then." Mrs. Johnson said as she stopped folding the laundry and went into the kitchen. Grant and I took seats at the kitchen table.

"Mom, where's the brats?"

"Your brothers and sister went with Big Momma this morning. She was taking them to some church function."

"Oh." Grant nervously spoke to his mother.

Mrs. Johnson stopped beating the eggs. "Since when have you been so concerned about your siblings' whereabouts?"

Grant shrugged his shoulders. "No reason. I was just wondering why it was so quiet."

Mrs. Johnson diverted her attention toward me. "Whatever, Grant. Unique, darling, are you feeling ill? Is that why Grant said you needed to eat?"

Mrs. Johnson retrieved the waffle iron from the bottom cabinet and gathered other items for our breakfast. She was completely oblivious to Grant and me as we moved from the kitchen table to the oversized island where she was washing a frying pan.

"Momma, there is something Unique and I need to tell you."

"Go ahead son. I can cook and listen at the same time. I am all yours."

"Well.... Momma.... uh...uh...Unique and I are going to get married next weekend."

Mrs. Johnson was taking extra eggs out of the refrigerator at the time. The eggs left her hand and spiraled quickly to the floor, cracking and splashing everywhere.

"What? What did you just tell me? Now I know I'm getting old but my hearing is apparently beginning to fail."

"Momma, you heard me. Unique and I are getting married, and..."

"Mrs. Johnson, I'm pregnant."

"Good, Lord. Lord, Jesus." Mrs. Johnson said as the glass-mixing bowel left her hands and shattered to the floor.

Her face became flushed. "I think I need to sit down. Son, hand me a glass of ice water."

"Yes Momma, right away."

"I must be delirious. You two are getting married next weekend and I'm going to be a grandmother? Grant, what...what are you going do about Stanford?"

"Momma, I can go to the University of Pittsburgh or Unique can move to California with me. I haven't figured everything out yet. But what I do know is I am extremely happy. I love her, Momma."

"Grant and Unique, marriage and a baby are colossal responsibilities. Neither one of them should be taken lightly. You two are moving very quickly. Have you truly thought about all of the ramifications this will have on your lives?"

"Yes Momma. My mind is made up. Why are you crying?" Grant moved toward his mother and embraced her with a loving hug.

Mrs. Johnson grabbed a tissue from the kitchen counter and wiped her eyes. "I'm crying because my baby is having a baby and he's getting married. Unique, we need to find you a wedding dress. Let's hurry up and eat breakfast. We need to go shopping as soon as possible."

I was shocked by Mrs. Johnson's generosity. "Oh...Mrs. Johnson, you don't hate me?"

"Unique, darling, I love as if you were one of my own and now you are going to be the mother of my grandchild. I am very upset but you didn't get pregnant all by yourself. Oh, my God…Justin's home. What in the world is he doing home so early?"

"Ingrid! Ingrid!" Mr. Johnson was in an enraged and yelling at the top of his lungs.

My legs shook and I felt like I was going to faint. "Grant, how could he know?"

Grant left his mother's side and walked toward me. "Unique, he couldn't know. But he's really pissed about something."

"Ingrid!"

"Justin, I'm in the kitchen. Please lower your voice. The windows are open and you're going to have all of the neighbors in our business."

"Damn, that bastard Morris Blackman. Have you seen the morning's paper?"

Mr. Johnson stopped dead in his tracks when he saw us in the kitchen.

"Hello, Mr. Johnson." I barely uttered.

Mr. Johnson's face was contorted with rage. "What the hell is she doing here?"

Grant turned to his father and blurted out, "Daddy, we are getting married next weekend and she's pregnant."

The dark complexion of Mr. Johnson's face turned bright red and his eyes narrowed. He looked like one of those demons I had seen in the spooky movies. You could feel the venom seeping out of his pores. He immediately left the kitchen and walked over to the small black coffee table that was located in the family room. He picked up the table and threw it against the French doors which led to the patio busting the panes of glass. Then he let out this outrageous guttural growl. "Grant, I am telling you the only way you are going to marry that bastard's daughter is over my dead body!"

Mr. Johnson frantically searched his pockets, pulled out his wallet, and tossed a wad of money at us. "Here, take this. It ought to be enough money to get an abortion."

I knew Mr. Johnson would be angry but his reaction was unforgivable. Instantaneously, I became hysterical. I ran out of the kitchen and out of the Johnson home. Grant was running right behind me.

*****

"Justin, I don't know what has gotten into you. You come in here shouting like a mad man and then you want to kill our grandchild! I'm sick of your mess, Justin, just sick of it. Your hatred with Morris has consumed you. I don't even know you anymore. Have you really taken a good look at our son lately? He and Unique are deeply in love! You need to accept it, move on, and live with it! Tell me Justin what did Morris Blackman do to you now?"

"Here read the morning's paper." Mr. Johnson said as he threw it at Mrs. Johnson's face.

"Oh…my sweet Jesus, he won't endorse you for the nomination of Mayor. My Lord, without his endorsement, you are just about finished."

"That bastard just won't let it go. He has been a thorn in my ass for over thirty years and now his daughter wants to ruin my son's life. There's no way in hell I tell you their marriage or pregnancy will ever take place! No way in hell!"

"Calm down Justin before your blood pressure goes through the roof and you have a heart attack."

"I'm going upstairs and lie down for a moment, Ingrid. I can't think straight. My head feels like a torpedo that is about to explode. When I get up, I expect you to have our son's ass and that girl here tonight so we can resolve this baby marriage issue. Justin is going to Stanford if I have to handcuff and fly him there myself!"

*****

"Oh, Grant we can't do this. Did you see how your father reacted? He detests my father and me. This will never work. I'll get an abortion and you can leave. We can just forget this nightmare."

"Unique, I'm not going anywhere! We need to go and call your father to make sure he is coming home tonight. We need to tell him. In the meantime, lets' go downtown to the City Hall building and get our marriage license."

"Are you absolutely sure you want to do this, Grant? I would understand if you changed your mind. Honestly, I would."

"Unique, I have loved you ever since you were a flat chested, no booty little girl. You and my baby are the most important people to me. Basketball isn't everything. Don't forget I have a 4.0 grade point average. I can go to any college. That's the least of my worries. Now move it. City Hall doesn't stay open forever.

Grant kissed me and walked me back to his house. We got in his car and head downtown. We had a wedding to plan.

After applying for our license, we stopped at the mall to purchase our gold wedding bands. The bands were very plain and simple but they symbolized so much more. We had just enough cash to pay for them. Grant used the money he saved for college. He made extra money by doing odd jobs for his family and by cutting the grass for some of the neighbors.

I was overwhelmed with the events of the day. I was finally filled with excitement and hope. I was starting to ascend up to cloud nine. I couldn't wait to share the news about my upcoming nuptials with Char and Ruby.

Grant and I walked out of the mall hand in hand I stopped and opened up the box that held our rings. I was mesmerized by our reflections which shined brightly in the gold bands.

"Grant these wedding bands are beautiful."

"I'm glad you like them. I'm sorry I didn't have enough money for a diamond engagement ring."

"Grant I don't care about any stupid diamond. The band is perfect."

"Well Unique, it may be perfect for now but once I go pro I'm going to surprise you with a big ole ten karat diamond."

"Really, Grant ten karats? Come on crazy, we need to step on it. My father should be home by now. Are you ready to face the music?"

"Let's roll baby cakes. We have God on our side. It's going to be okay."

The drive home to my house was very peaceful. Surprisingly, my Daddy honored my request and came home.

"Well Grant, he's home. Are you ready?"

"As ready as I'm ever going to be. I love you Unique."

"I love you too."

I inserted the key into the door and Daddy was sitting in his favorite tattered chair watching the evening news.

"Hi Daddy."

Daddy peered over his glasses, looked at Grant, and sucked his teeth before he spoke. "Hey."

Grant walked over to Daddy and politely spoke, "Hello, Mr. Blackman." He extended his hand to Daddy. Daddy didn't shake Grant's hand. He just continued to stare at him.

Then he spoke. "Hello, Grant. Unique, what do you want to tell me? I know whatever it is must be extremely important because you never call me at work."

"Uh...Daddy, I don't know where to begin. Well...I...I...um...went to the doctor's office the other day. They found a small tumor on my fallopian tubes and...I'm...I'm... going to have a baby."

My Daddy looked at us. Then he quickly rose from his chair and started to walk toward me. He raised his fist to hit me but Grant caught his fist right before it connected with my face.

"Boy, you better get the hell up off of me."

"I'm sorry Sir, but you will never ever put your hands on Unique again. We are getting married next weekend and we are going to have our child. She won't be your property any more. If you hurt her before our wedding, I'll have to kill you."

An eerie demented laugh escaped from my father. "Grant you're a sorry pathetic boy just like you damn father, Justin Ellington Johnson. I see the apple doesn't fall far from the tree."

"Daddy, how did you know who Grant's father is? You have never met his parents before."

"Unique, don't be so naïve, girl. Do you really think I thought you were always running over to Char or Ruby house? Child, please don't be so stupid. I knew some Negro had your nose wide open. Don't forget I am the mayor soon to be the governor of this great state of Pennsylvania. I know everything that goes on in this neighborhood. I have connections. Besides, the bastard looks just like his black father, Little Brother Shit A Lot."

"Daddy, stop it! Stop it right now! How can you be so damn rude?"

"It's okay Unique, I don't have to stand here and listen to your father. My father is by far a better man than your father will ever be."

"Boy, you sound just like your pathetic daddy. Go ask him about his college days. We have a very tight bond. I hate him just as much as he hates me. Now get the fuck out of my house. Unique, you stay here."

"Sorry, Daddy, but I'm going with Grant."

"Fine! I see you have made your bed, now wallow in it and get the fuck out!"

We were very distraught after our conversation with Daddy. Both of our fathers' reactions caught us off guard. It was worse than we had anticipated. We didn't want to go home so we put the last of our money together and got a hotel room for the night. A good night's rest and making sweet love are just what we both needed.

"Tomorrow we need to get up early and look for an apartment. Then I need to look for another part time job. It's not going to be easy, Unique, but as long as you're by my side we can conquer the world. Are you with me?"

"I'm with you."

After making love, we fell asleep wrapped in each other's embrace, looking forward to our new future with the belief all would be right with the world.

Chapter 9

Morris Blackman went to sleep in a foul mood and woke up the next morning in an even fouler one. The news of his daughter's impending wedding and her becoming a mother had taken its toll. A temporary moment of guilt crept into his thoughts, "Maybe, I should have paid more attention to her." He shrugged his shoulders to dismiss his absurd feelings and proceeded to walk into the bathroom. He took a shower, shaved, got dressed, grabbed his briefcase, and snatched his keys off of the dresser. He exited the front door and got into his car like he did every morning.

He stopped at Eat N Park on Washington Boulevard. It was one of his favorite places to eat. He patronized the restaurant regularly. The employees adored him and they felt honored to have a celebrity in their presence. Of course Morris loved the attention he received from the young doting waitresses who were always at his beck and call.

He sat in the same booth every day, the one that was located in the back of the restaurant by the window which faced the parking lot. He ordered his usual breakfast two pancakes, scrambled eggs, a small bowl of grits, three slices of extra crispy bacon, a large glass of orange juice, and a cup of black coffee. He perused the New York Times, The Pittsburgh Courier as well as the Pittsburgh Post Gazette. Morris Blackman was positive Justin Ellington Johnson's short-lived mayoral race was down the tubes and he was very pleased with himself.

*****

Justin Ellington Johnson had a restless night. He tossed and turned all night trying to get comfortable but it was to no avail. He had a severe migraine that awakened him earlier than usual. He sat on the edge of the bed, closed his eyes, exhaled, and prayed his oldest son was not going to be a father. He sighed, deciding to just get up and start his day.

He kissed Ingrid on the forehead, grabbed his migraine medication off of the nightstand, and proceeded down the hallway so he could check on the triplets. He peered through the cracked bedroom door and there they were sleeping like little angels, not a care or worry in the world. Justin wished he didn't have any worries but he did. He went downstairs to the kitchen and made some coffee. He had such a feeling of despair. His worst nightmare was now an actuality. His son was going to marry the daughter of the one man on this earth who he truly loathed. Now his archenemy was going to be tied to him for the rest of his life. It was hard to fathom his first grandchild was going to be part Morris Blackman. Justin felt very bleak. His political career was, in essence finished and his son was going to be ruined by Morris Blackman just like he was. No, history was not going to repeat itself and that was for damn sure.

After finishing his coffee, Justin went back upstairs. He tried to lay back down to get some much-needed rest but he had other things on his mind. He got back up and went into the bathroom so he could take a shower. Perhaps the pulsating hot water would ease the tension which was pulling at the base of his neck.

After his shower, Justin shaved, combed his hair, and got dressed. While his family still slept, he again kissed his wife and his youngest children goodbye. He whispered in their ears, "Remember I love you." He descended down the steps that led to the living room, grabbed his keys off of the television set and walked out the door. He had to talk to Blackman today, first thing. He wasn't sure what he would say or do but he knew something had to be done. Today would be the last time Morris Blackman snubbed his nose at him or his family!

****

Morris Blackman arrived at his office around nine thirty on a sunny Tuesday morning. His secretary, Mrs. Norelle, a long time and dedicated employee of the Mayor handed him his messages. They exchanged the usual pleasantries. He smiled then entered his plush office. He surveyed each note. "Damn, each message is from that bastard Johnson." He said to no one in particular. He figured he would be hearing from Johnson soon, but later would have been better. Morris was barely seated when Mrs. Norelle buzzed him on his intercom.

"What is it? Mrs. Norelle."

"Mr. Mayor, Judge Johnson is here to see you but he doesn't have an appointment. Should I schedule one?"

"No need to schedule an appointment, send him in. Thanks, Mrs. Norelle."

"You are welcome, Mr. Mayor."

Blackman's security guard, George, led Judge Johnson to the Mayor's office. The guard thought to himself that the Judge seemed exceptionally nervous. Justin's face was very stern and cold. He kept fidgeting with something in his right pocket as he kept pace with the guard.

The guard knocked on Blackman's door. "Excuse me, Mr. Mayor; I've escorted Judge Johnson to see you. Would you like me to search him?"

"That won't be necessary George. I'm sure the Honorable Judge Johnson has nothing to hide. Besides, we go way back. We're fraternity brothers."

"Okay, Mr. Mayor. I'll be right outside your door if you need anything." Something just didn't feel right to George but the Mayor seemed confident enough for him not to search this Judge Johnson. George worked for the Mayor for nearly nine years and never remembered seeing Judge Johnson paying a visit to the Mayor.

"Thank you, George."

George nodded and left the Mayor's office. He stood outside the Mayor's door with his hand slightly on his gun. This was George's usual stance when his gut told him something was terribly wrong.

"Justin, sit down and make yourself comfortable. I've been expecting you. It's my understanding after all of these years we are going to be family. Grandfathers too, that sounds like a cause for a celebration. Would you like a cigar? They're Cuban, you know? It's funny how fate keeps throwing us together."

An agitated Justin wrung his hands and wiped perspiration from his upper lip. "Don't patronize me, you bastard."

"Come now, Justin, lower your voice. Someone like George might think you have some type of animosity toward me and that wouldn't be a good thing."

"Morris, listen to me. You have to get your daughter to have an abortion and to leave my son alone. Grant has such a bright future ahead of him, a full ride at Stanford to play basketball. I will not allow your daughter to ruin my son's life, like you ruined my life and Jenny's."

Morris let out an eerie laugh. "Justin, Justin, Justin, don't tell me after all of these years you are still harboring feelings for my poor deceased wife? Come now, that was such a long time ago. You really need to get your life in order. I think all of your focus should be directed toward that fine voluptuous wife of yours. How is Ingrid these days?"

Morris's arrogant comment was the last straw for Johnson. He leaped out of his chair, and walked towards Blackman who was seated behind an oversized mahogany desk. Johnson was very frantic and shouted at Blackman, "You pompous bastard! Don't you dare utter my wife's name! You have ruined me for the last time, you turncoat motherfucker!"

"Sit down Justin! You are making a fool of yourself."

Justin ignored Morris's request, walked around Morris's desk and stood directly in front of his nemesis. He continued to shout at Morris. "Yeah, I'll be your fool."

On the other side of the door, George heard the yelling between the Mayor and the Judge. He opened up the Mayor's door to see Judge Johnson in Blackman's face. Immediately he interrupted them. "Sir, are you okay?"

Morris pushed himself in his chair, allowing himself to move closer to the wall and away from Johnson. "Yes, George, I'm fine. Judge Johnson was just expressing his frustration about a current predicament we both are experiencing. I'm sure the situation can be resolved momentarily. We are going to work everything out. Trust me, George, I'm just fine."

"Okay, sir. I'm just outside your door if you need me."

"I'll keep that in mind. Thank you, George."

George nodded at the Mayor and slowly closed the door. His instincts were working overtime telling him to stay very close. He followed his gut instincts, grabbed his radio, and called two other guards, just in case something should jump off.

"I can honestly say Morris I hate you. I really don't think the word hate accurately describes my feelings for you. Despise and detest are probably closer to my true thoughts. You have been a bastard all of your life. And I can bet my last dollar you killed Jenny. You beat her all of the time."

"Why Justin, how would you know what went on at my house? I believe that falls under privileged information. I took great precautions to ensure my marriage was kept confidential and not made public to the outside world. Tell me Your Honor, were you fucking my wife?"

"Why you prick!" Johnson yelled. He then reached into his right pocket and whipped out a black thirty-eight revolver and pointed the gun at Blackman's head.

George's internal radar went off. He decided to open the Mayor's door. What George saw terrified him and chilled him deep down in his bones. "Judge Johnson! Put the gun down nice and slow! We don't want anyone to get hurt."

A nervous Johnson waved the gun in front of Blackman's face. "Tell him to leave Morris. Tell him right now, or I swear to God I will splatter your brains all across this room."

Blackman's voice seemed to quiver. George, put the gun down. I'm sure we can work this out. Isn't that right, Judge?"

George took at step toward the Mayor. "Sorry, sir, I can't do that." By then, two more guards appeared in the Mayor's office with guns pointed toward the Judge.

Johnson started weeping as he continued to point the gun at Blackman's head. "I hate you! God only knows how much I hate you."

Realizing Justin had lost it, Blackman started to squirm and perspire. Sweat started to formulate on his forehead and he could feel his heart racing. Blackman's "Ah ha" moment came as he realized his past actions had more ramifications than he ever anticipated. He never counted on Johnson being unstable and never counted on seeing the years of torture and hatred which was reflected in Johnson's soulless dark eyes.

Blackman tried to gather his thoughts before he spoke as he realized how volatile the situation had become. "Justin, listen to me I…I apologize for all the hurt I have caused you. Think about your wife and your children. Do you really want them to remember you as a murderer? Just put the gun down. I'm sure we can work this out. I'll even call a news conference and endorse you as the next Mayor. Yeah…I can do that just put the gun down."

"Just… just shut the fuck up! Morris. It's too late for an apology. You would sell your own daughter if you thought you could get out of this but you can't! It ends today! DO YOU HEAR ME? IT ENDS TODAY!"

Johnson was so close to Blackman's face the sweat from his brow dropped on Blackman's upper lip. Blackman was sweating profusely. Perspiration started to leak through his crisp, lightly starched white shirt. He felt a tightening in his chest as he tried to plead for his life.

"Justin my main man put the gun down. Look, forget about the news conference. If you don't want my endorsement I…I will need new staff when I become governor and I know I can find a high power position for you. Perhaps I can put you on the ballot as Lieutenant Governor, wouldn't you like that?"

"Morris, you are fucking unbelievable! Do you think you can just buy me? You don't know me at all. Oh…that's right you never tried to know me. Now did you? You just made my life miserable because of the color of my skin. In your eyes I was not good enough because I wasn't high yellow and passing for white. You ostracized me. I was an outcast in my own fraternity. Morris how can you hate your own? Answer me how can you hate me?"

"Justin, that's ridiculous. It's not true. You are not thinking straight. Listen to me if you want money name your price I can give you whatever you want just name it."

"Shut up Morris! Just shut up! I don't want to hear anymore of your lies. I want you to take a good long look at this black man because I will be the last man you will ever see. I hope my face haunts you in hell."

Johnson continued to wave the gun back and forth in Blackman's face like he was a crazed madman.

George and the other two guards slowly and systematically moved in closer to the assailant and the Mayor. Judge Johnson was in such a state of hopelessness he didn't notice the approaching guards. George again raised his voice in a last ditch effort to save the Mayor. "For the last time, your Honor I need you to put the gun down!"

"Justin, please…I'm begging you. Is that what you want me to do? Well, I'm begging you not to do this. Think about your family. What would Jenny want you to do?"

"Don't you dare speak to me about Jenny! Do you really know what you are Blackman? You're a murdering, lying, manipulating, cunning son of a bitch! I think the world has had enough of the great Morris Blackman the third. No more, you bastard! I should have done this to you a long time ago. God forgive me."

"Noooooo…" George shouted.

In a flash, the Honorable Justin Ellington Johnson shot Mayor Morris Blackman the third in the head as the guards riddled the Judge's body with bullets.

Bullets flew inside the Mayor's office; chaos broke out in the hallway. Horrific, deafening, and terrifying screams could be heard from Mrs. Norelle and the other administrative staff as they ran for cover.

By ten o'clock, on a bright and sunny Tuesday morning, two lives were gone and two families would be forever changed by the day's event.

George ran to the Mayor's side and yelled at the other guards, "Call an ambulance and get the paramedics in here now!" He turned and cuddled the Mayor in his arms and said, "Hold on Mr. Mayor, hold on." George who was in a state of shock failed to realize it was too late. The Mayor's splattered brains were now apart of the office wall décor. George cried as he watched Blackman gurgle and take his last breath as dark crimson blood continued to flow from the Mayor's lifeless body onto the floor.

Pandemonium broke out as news crews got wind of the Mayor's untimely demise by the hands of a Judge who was also dead.

Chapter 10

Across town oblivious to the morning's events, Grant and I awakened in each other's arms as the bright sunshine flowed through the closed curtains in our sleazy hotel room.

"Good morning, my love." Grant said as he kissed me tenderly on my lips.

"Good morning, Grant. I can't believe you snored all night long. Then you made some unbelievable noises. I barely got any sleep."

"I hate to tell you, Miss Blackman, it was you who was calling on the pigs last night, not me. I hope you don't snore like that until you deliver. I'll never get any rest."

"You've got a lot of nerve. I am telling the truth, it wasn't me." I said as I hit Grant with a pillow. We laughed as I reached for the remote control and turned on the television.

Across the TV, the words flashed "Special Report."

"Turn up the TV, Unique. Look at all of those cops. It looks like something big is happening. I think they are downtown."

"Yeah, it sure looks like it. I bet it's a bank robbery and someone was murdered."

"Be quiet, Unique. The news anchor Wilson Pratt, Pratt Wilson, or whatever his name is, is about to speak. Turn the volume up."

"Dag… Grant, are you deaf, you really need to get your hearing checked."

"Be quiet, Unique."

"Whatever, Grant."

"This is Pratt Wilson Channel Two News reporting to you live from downtown Pittsburgh in front of the City County Building. We are breaking into regularly scheduled broadcasting this morning to bring you this unraveling story. Channel Two News has confirmed reports there has been a shooting inside the Mayor's office. Details of exactly what has happened are still unfolding at this time."

"Oh…my God, Daddy…" I softly as I looked at Grant in disbelief.

Pratt Wilson continued to speak. "In just a few moments we will be hearing from Police Chief Eric Homes who will give us an update of the situation. Again, if you are just tuning in, let's bring you up to speed. There have been reports that shots have been fired in the Mayor's office. We are uncertain as of ye if anyone is wounded, or if the Mayor is okay. We're getting reports stating Mayor Blackman is the one who has been gun down. We are unclear if the Mayor has suffered severe or life threatening his injuries. The Mayor's office has been tight lipped and has not a released an official statement. Thus far, these reports have been unsubstantiated."

Swiftly, the handsome, distinguished looking and the youngest Pittsburgh Police Chief, Eric Homes came out of the County Building and approached the podium. He adjusted the microphone as frenzied reporters yelled to him. He wore a grave look. He took a deep breath and exhaled. He again adjusted the microphone. He looked at the crowd intently as he waited for the reporters to calm down.

"Chief Homes!" Reporter one yelled.

"Chief!" Pratt Wilson shouted from the crowd as he thrust another microphone in the Chief's face. "Chief, can you confirm the reports that it is the Mayor who was shot."

"No! It can't be!" I shouted as I sat at the edge of the bed holding on to Grant for dear life.

Police Chief Homes' deep and authoritative voice ripped through the crowd of reporters. Immediately, the conversing amongst the restless reporters ceased. "I have some very unfortunate and sad news to report. Today, at approximately 10:15 a.m. our beloved Mayor…Mayor Morris Blackman was assassinated."

Sighs of disbelief reverberated throughout the crowd. As Police Chief Homes continued his statement to the press I screamed at the top of my lungs. "No…!"

"The assailant has been identified as Judge Justin Ellington Johnson. Eyewitnesses have given their statements which confirmed Judge Johnson was at the Mayor's office early this morning. The Mayor and the Judge had some sort of confrontation which could be heard outside the Mayor's office. This altercation alerted the Mayor's guard, George McDonald, who then summoned two other guards. While waiting for the other guards to arrive, Mr. McDonald opened the Mayor's office door and asked the Mayor if everything was okay. The Mayor advised him, he and the Judge were having a disagreement. The other two guards arrived and they stood posted outside the Mayor's door until they heard Judge Johnson's voice becoming very animated and outraged. Upon opening the door to the Mayor's office, Mr. McDonald saw Judge Johnson waving a gun in the Mayor's face. The guards quickly drew their weapons and the Judge was ordered to stand down. The Judge ignored their commands and proceeded to shoot the Mayor point blank in the head. The guards opened fire on the Judge, hitting him multiple times. Mr. McDonald called for an ambulance but it was too late. Unfortunately, both men were pronounced dead at the scene of this horrendous crime."

The news personnel talked amongst themselves. All of them were in a state of confusion and disbelief. They shouted at the Chief again.

At the hotel, Grant and I held each other. Grant was crying uncontrollably but I remained tearless.

"Grant, let go of me. I need to use the bathroom."

I ran to the bathroom where I continually heaved and hurled until green bile flowed from my mouth. I lay down on the floor in a fetal position as I waited for the room to stop spinning. Grant didn't come into the bathroom to see if I was all right.

I managed to pull myself up to the sink. I rinsed my mouth out with cold water and splashed some on my face. I returned to the bed to find Grant still staring at the television.

Pratt Wilson, the newest member of the Channel Two News team was frantically trying to obtain the Chief's attention. Pratt Wilson was positive he could get an exclusive interview with the Chief. Getting the interview would definitely be a feather in his hat. It would secure his position as one of the best newscasters in the business. He proceeded to yell at the Chief. "Police Chief Holmes."

"Yes, Pratt?"

"Do you have a motive at this time?"

"At this time, we don't have a motive. We are still in the process of questioning the rest of the Mayor's staff, guards, and other personnel who were at work this morning."

Pratt Wilson continued, "Chief, everyone knows the Mayor wouldn't endorse Judge Johnson as the next Mayor of Pittsburgh. Could that be why they were arguing?"

Police Chief Homes seemed a bit irritated by Pratt Wilson. "As I stated before Mr. Wilson, we do not have a motive at this time. This is an active investigation and we have to speak with everyone who was working at the Mayor's office before we could draw any conclusions about any disagreements."

"Police Chief Homes!" Reporter one yelled again.

"Chief! Chief!" The news reporters screamed again.

Police Chief Homes looked out to the crowd of crazed reporters and said "I have no further comments. We should have more details later in the day. I will have another news conference this afternoon around three. Thank you." The Police Chief Homes turned to his right and headed back to the crime scene leaving the hysterical reporters.

Pratt Wilson composed himself and spoke eloquently to the camera. "This is Pratt Wilson Channel Two News. We will break into regularly scheduled programming as events unfold in this bizarre but very sad story. It's a heartrending day for the citizens of Pittsburgh. Our prayers go out to the families of Mayor Blackman and Judge Johnson. We will return you to The Guiding Light."

Grant was crying uncontrollably. I got dressed and then I helped Grant. He was so distraught he was barely able to speak.

"Come on, Grant. We need to get home to your mother."

"Unique. My…my…dad, he's…he's gone."

"I know Grant and so is my Daddy. Let's go. I'll drive home."

"Okay." Grant said as he helplessly walked toward the car.

It took us thirty-five minutes to get home. The streets were filled to capacity with news trucks, cameras, and reporters.

I honked the horn so we could pull into the driveway of Grant's house. Before we could get out of the car, the reporters descended on us like vultures attacking its prey. As we pushed through the first level of reporters, another group shouted at us, "Aren't you Grant Johnson, the Judge's son and you…you are the Mayor's daughter, correct?"

"No comment!" I screamed as I continued to push our way through the crowd. I dragged the despondent Grant behind me. The reporters followed us up the walkway and up the steps that led to the Johnson's front door. I nervously took Grant's key out of his pocket. The screaming reporters had me so unnerved I dropped the keys on the patio. Distressed, I picked the keys up and haphazardly jiggled them in the keyhole until the door finally opened. I looked out to the reporters and slammed the door in their faces.

Once we got inside the house, I took a deep breath and gathered my thoughts. I was really rattled by all the media attention. Sure, I have done press conferences with my father but nothing had prepared me for the chaotic reporters.

Grant and I could hear voices coming from the back of the house. We walked slowly toward the usually bright and cheerful Johnson family room to find a sullen and tearful, Mrs. Johnson, the triplets, and Big Momma. All of them were huddled together in a sad embrace.

Mrs. Johnson sprang to her feet. "Grant I was worried about you. Where in the world have you been?" Mrs. Johnson said in between her cries. She got up from the couch, walked over and grabbed Grant.

"Your daddy is gone. Oh, sweet Jesus, your daddy is gone. Unique, I'm so sorry, baby." Mrs. Johnson held us tight. Big Momma was holding the wailing triplets in her arms.

"Mrs. Johnson, it's not your fault. You don't have to apologize. I just don't understand. Why did Mr. Johnson hate my Daddy so much? Mrs. Johnson, I think something is wrong with Grant. He hasn't said a word since we got in the car and that's been almost an hour."

Mrs. Johnson took Grants' hand and pulled him. "Oh...Unique, I'll answer all of your questions but I need to take care of my son first. I believe Grant, is in shock. Here, let's lay him down on the sofa. Grant baby, we are going to get through this together. You hear me boy."

Grant stared at his momma as tears fluently poured from his eyes. Mrs. Johnson kissed Grant on the forehead and covered him with a blanket. She gestured for me to sit down on the other end of the couch.

"Unique, honey, I don't know where to begin."

"Mrs. Johnson, you should just start at the beginning." I said very dryly.

For over an hour, Mrs. Johnson told me of the hatred my father and Mr. Johnson harbored for each other. It was unconceivable to me that two educated and intelligent men could hold such spite and hatred toward each other for over thirty years. I found it remarkable someone could actually detest another human being for so long.

I felt like this situation was entirely my fault. If I had the abortion like Char had advised me then Grant would be one plane ride away from Stanford. I would be off to Spelman with Char and Ruby and our fathers would still be alive.

The doorbell at the Johnson's home rang nonstop. The reporters were not going to give up until they received a statement from the grieving family.

"I've had enough of this!" Big Momma angrily stated as she proceeded to the front door. Big Momma was a very large woman. She was as wide as she was tall. She had a powerful stride and with each step Big Momma took to reach the front door the entire house seemed to succumb to her heavy feet as they vibrated on the hardwood floors.

She reached the entrance in a matter of moments. When she opened the door, she found the face of Pratt Wilson who stood in her space. Big Momma mustered up all of her strength and furiously spewed at the reporters. "No comment at this time!"

Before Pratt Wilson could utter a word, Big Momma had slammed the door right in his face. "Ahh…I feel a little better," she said to herself as she returned to the family room.

A grim look spread across Mrs. Johnson face when she unexpectedly got up from the couch. She grabbed us and headed toward the front door. When Mrs. Johnson opened the front door, the reporters went wild.

Reporter one yelled, "There she is! Mrs. Johnson!"

Mrs. Johnson stood on the front porch looking very frail and rattled. She pushed away a piece of her swooped bang. She straightened and smoothed out her dress even though there were no apparent wrinkles in sight. The tears Mrs. Johnson shed all morning caused her usually striking eyes to become red and puffy. The essence of a beautiful woman was still apparent even though Mrs. Johnson's eyes were almost swollen shut from the weeping.

Mrs. Johnson looked out to the maddening reporters, microphones, lights, and cameras. She cleared her throat and wiped the tears from her eyes before speaking to the eager crowd of reporters. "I find it hard to express to you…how to explain too you…um…how our family is dealing with this unbearable grief that is ripping at every inch of our heart. However, I felt it necessary at this time to come out here and address all of you in hopes when I am finished you will leave us alone so we may digest the events of the day. Our family is very overwhelmed and distraught over the killing of the mayor by my husband, Judge Justin Johnson. My husband left behind a loving mother-in-law, four loving children he adored, and a dedicated wife. The Mayor is survived by his only child, a daughter who is standing here next to me on my right. My husband and the Mayor hated each other for over thirty years. Today it ended. My son, Grant and the Mayor's daughter, Unique are going to get married and start their own family. It's time for these two families to heal. I am praying the past will be buried with my husband and the Mayor. I hope and pray in the afterlife my husband and the Mayor can find peace and forgiveness."

Mrs. Johnson paused to wipe her rolling tears. The crowd of reporters calmed down and quietly waited for Mrs. Johnson to utter her next words.

"I am requesting my husband and the Mayor's funeral be held together so there can be at last a resolution to this unspeakable nightmare. I am requesting all of you leave now and let us mourn in peace. I won't be issuing any more statements so please leave us alone. Thank you."

Mayhem broke out as the reporters screamed at Mrs. Johnson for more questions. Big Momma gladly shut the door in their faces.

As soon as Char and Ruby heard the news, they came running over Grant's house. They walked me down to my house to get some clothes. Mrs. Johnson didn't want me to stay home by myself, so I stayed in their guest bedroom.

"Unique."

"Yes, Char?"

"Well…I…I haven't seen you shed a tear are you okay?"

"I don't know. It's like I know he's not coming back but some how I feel relieved. Is that normal?"

"I don't know", said Ruby.

"If it was my dad, I would be hysterical," said Char.

"Me too," Ruby chimed in.

"Look you two. I appreciate you being here but I'm exhausted. I'm going to check in on Grant and go to bed."

"Okay. We'll come up tomorrow. If you need anything just, call us," said Char as she gave me an enduring hug.

"That's right girl, we've got your back. I hope Grant comes around. Ruby said as tears left her eyes.

I hugged my girls. "I know you love me. The doctor said Grant is in shock. He really loved his father and I think he blames me too. You know he barley looks at me. Maybe, I will get rid of this baby."

The three of us were so engrossed in our conversation we did not notice Mrs. Johnson had descended from the upstairs bedroom and was now eavesdropping in our conversation.

"You will not get rid of my grandchild," said Mrs. Johnson.

"Ooooh…Mrs. Johnson. I…I…didn't know that you were standing there."

"Go on home, girls. Unique and I need to have a talk."

Mrs. Johnson gave Ruby and Char a very stern look through her swollen eyes.

"Goodnight, Unique, Mrs. Johnson." They said in unison.

"Goodnight." Mrs. Johnson said as she walked the girls out.

"Unique, my dear, dear Unique. My husband lost his mind over this grandchild and I forbid you to get rid of this baby. This baby is apart of him too. You get that foolishness out of your head right this instance. Do you hear me?"

"Yes, Mrs. Johnson, I hear you. But…"

"But…nothing. All you need is a good night's sleep. You go on up to bed. Good night, my dear."

"Good night, Mrs. Johnson."

Before I retired, I walked down the long winding corridors that led to Grant's room. I guess the sedative the doctor gave Grant finally worked. He looked so peaceful like he didn't have a care in the world. I wish I could take a pill. Sleep was the last thing on my mind. I walked over to Grant and planted a soft kiss on his forehead. I whispered in his ear, "Tomorrow, is another day my love." I turned out his bedroom light and I proceeded to go upstairs to bed, still not sure of what I felt. Not sure of what the next couple of days would bring.

Chapter 11

The press kept their distance as Mrs. Johnson had requested but they still managed to follow Grant, Mrs. Johnson, and me as we went to the funeral home to prepare the final arrangements for our father's funeral. We picked out the caskets and flowers that would decorate them.

After two days of silence, Grant was finally coming around. He expressed his love for me and was now more determined than ever to make our family work.

As the day approached that we buried my father and Mr. Johnson. I still had not shed a tear for my father nor had one dropped for Mr. Johnson. Have I become so cold and heartless? What was wrong with me?

As we drove to the church for the funeral, I just stared out the window. I couldn't bear to look in the Johnson family's eyes. All sorts of feelings were running through my mind. To my amazement, I saw a bright beautiful rainbow in the sky. It reminded me of what my momma told me. She said when you saw a rainbow in the sky it signified that the storm was over. At that instance, the week's events hit me like a ton of bricks. I broke down and cry. I wailed like there was no tomorrow which caused a chain reaction in all of the passengers in the limousine. By the time, we arrived at the church all of us were emotionally worn out.

Mrs. Johnson pulled me close. "Now, now my dear, Unique it's going to be all right. I promise you. Calm down before you make yourself sick."

"I'll try, Mrs. Johnson."

"I know you will, my dear."

The limousine stopped in front of the church. Both sides of the street were filled with news reporters and their equipment. There was a long line of people going up the steps of the cathedral. All of them waited to pay their last respects to Daddy and the Judge.

The chauffer opened the door to the limo so we could get out and start the long walk of the funeral procession.

Once we arrived inside the entrance of the church, I asked the Funeral Director if I could see my Daddy one last time. He stated Mrs. Johnson requested the bodies be rolled into the front of the church once the family arrived so I had a few moments to spare before the ceremony officially began. He pointed me in the direction of the room where my father's body rested.

I slowly entered the dimly lit room. The room was modest in its furnishings. There was one beaten and worn black leather chair situated in the corner of the room. There was an oval glass table with one lit candle which smelled of fresh gardenias. The Lord's Prayer was in a gold frame and was placed on the wall which faced my Daddy's coffin. My knees buckled as I made my way to the lifeless body of my Daddy. Daddy was in a silver casket that was trimmed in gold. Since Daddy had served in the Korean War. I opted to have United States flag draped on his coffin in lieu of flowers. Besides, Daddy wasn't much into flowers. I dressed Daddy in his favorite attire a black pinstriped suit with a white shirt and a black silk tie with tiny maroon stripes.

I took the flag off of the coffin and carefully opened the lid. I stood there and took a long look at him. I looked at my Daddy as if it were the first time. Nowhere, did I see the bullet hole that ended my father's life. The funeral home did an exceptional job at making my father look like he was taking a nap. Strangely enough, he looked at peace.

I took out a piece of paper from my purse. I was awakened early this morning with a poem in my heart for Daddy. I wanted to write something for him so he would know exactly how I felt. Too bad I couldn't face him with these words when he was alive. Oh well…better late than never.

I read it out loud making sure he didn't miss a word. I must be crazy. He can't really hear me. Can he? Perhaps on his journey to the afterlife the wind will carry my voice to his ears.

"Dear Daddy, I never really expressed my true feelings to you so I wrote this poem for you. It's called For Today I Cry.

For Today I Cry because today is the day that I bury my father.

For Today I Cry because I will not miss you nearly as much as I long for and wish for my mother's touch.

For Today I Cry for all of the years of abuse that my mother and I endured by your hand.

For Today I Cry because I came to realize that you never took the time to really know me.

For Today I Cry because I'm in conflict and I am filled with all sorts of emotion.

For Today I Cry as I comprehend that you will never get to see the baby that moves in my belly.

For Today I Cry because you will never walk me down the aisle.

For Today I Cry as I grasp at the thought that you will never get the chance to see the woman I have become.

For Today I Cry as I realize all the hopes and dreams I had of us ever becoming close have vanished right before my eyes.

For Today I Cry because now I am an orphan.

For Today I Cry as I ask God to forgive me.

For Today I Cry because apart of me is overjoyed that you are dead.

For Today I Cry because I cannot wish that you rest in peace.

For Today I Cry because I wish and I pray you will miss the pearly gates and go straight to HELL!

For Today I Cry.

Your one and only,

Unique."

With that, I folded up the piece of paper and placed it in the inside pocket of my father's suit. I gently closed the lid, draped the flag back over the coffin, walked out the door, and stood in line with the Johnsons as we waited for the funeral procession to begin.

Chapter 12

A few months passed since Grant and I buried our fathers. I continued to stay at my house alone, as I had done previously on so many nights before my father's death.

Grant got accepted to the University of Pittsburgh on a full basketball scholarship. He stayed on campus and occasionally stayed with me on the weekends. Staying alone in the house now felt very odd to me. I guess the finality of Daddy not walking in the front door at any moment had finally sunked in.

Daddy had an insurance policy which paid off the little amount of mortgage he still owed. The house was officially mine free and clear. His last will and testament stated he left me three hundred and fifty thousand dollars. I am in complete shock. I never expected any inheritance. I always thought he would leave his money to one of his girl friends or an animal shelter or something. I never thought he cared enough to leave me anything. In Daddy's own twisted way, he did have a heart that held some type of love for me. I only wish he could have conveyed his love to me in the true way a father loves his girl. Maybe, next lifetime we will get a chance to make our relationship right.

Grant was busy preparing for his first semester. He decided to take pre- law classes just in case the basketball gig didn't work out. At least he was being proactive by thinking about another lucrative career which could provide great income potential. I admired him for that. There were so many young men out in the world who truly believed they couldn't have a decent life if they didn't play ball. Well at least, Grant would be able to interrupt his own contracts should he go pro. Even though Grant's dream of attending Stanford was a dream deferred I believe for the most part, he was actually happy to be close to home.

At night he picked up a part-time job at Burger King. This allowed him the flexibility to work between basketball practice, basketball games, and studying. He was determined to somehow take care of the baby and me on his own. I told him not to worry because the money my daddy left me would go a long way but he didn't want me to use up my inheritance.

Grant and I decided to use some of my money but it was for a good cause. I have to admit we did splurge a little; we traded in my daddy's car Grant's old Chevy Nova and purchased two new Honda Civics. We didn't go overboard. We took the extra money and started a savings account. Mrs. Johnson flipped out when she saw the cars but hey, it wasn't her money.

Mrs. Johnson pulled some strings at the downtown bank where she worked and got me a job as a bank teller. Surprisingly, I actually enjoyed working. It was a great experience to work with so many diverse people. Each day was a new adventure. I also received a great benefit package that included health and dental insurance as well as a retirement account. I was so happy I didn't have to worry about health or dental insurance. My baby was going to have everything she or he needed. I hoped I had a girl because all of the baby clothes were so cute and pink. All in all my life was starting to shape up.

I had to confess, I was a little dejected when Ruby and Char left for Spelman. We had so many plans and dreams we were going to share together. Char, Ruby, and I were going to take Spelman by storm. Atlanta would never be the same after we left our mark on the Georgia peach. Oh well…with life there is always changes besides it was my choice to become a mother. There was really no reason to shed any tears for my destiny had already been decided.

I had just finished cleaning the house when there was a knock at the door. I wasn't expecting Grant until later on in the afternoon. I opened the door and found Mrs. Johnson and Grant standing on the porch.

"Grant, Mrs. Johnson, what are you two doing here?" I said as I opened the screen door and ushered them in.

Grant kissed me on the forehead and winked at me. "Well, Miss Unique, we came to plan our wedding."

"What? Plan our wedding? What is going on?"

"My mother called me last night and told me I had to be home so here I am."

Mrs. Johnson looked around the living room and proceeded to sit down on the couch. She coughed before she spoke. "Unique, dear, I'm well aware on the weekends you and Grant have been keeping or should I say playing house. You two are in here fornicating living in sin and then halfway going to church on Sunday. I cannot stand by with a clear conscience and do nothing about this situation. I won't allow it anymore. I'm on the Board of Trustees for heaven's sake. Our family's reputation is far from stellar and we need to change your living situation as soon as possible. I contacted the church to see if Pastor Clemmons was available to preside over the nuptials. Unfortunately, Pastor is on vacation, so I contacted the next best person to officiate the celebration. I've talked to a very good friend of mine Judge Randall Houston. As a favor to me the Judge has cleared his schedule and is available to preside over the ceremony next Saturday at three."

"Next Saturday? Grant, are you okay with this? It's all happening extremely fast. I don't even have a dress. Where are we going to have the wedding? I thought we were just going to go downtown to the Justice of the Peace."

"Well, Unique..." That was all Grant could say because Mrs. Johnson took over the conversation.

"Don't worry Unique, we can go shopping today. I've cancelled all of my appointments so I am at your disposal. I wrote all of today's activities in my planner."

I sat on the couch next to Grant trying to wrap my head around this wedding. A wedding which was going to occur on Saturday and I was so unprepared. I nudged Grant.

"Grant...your mom, what is she doing?"

"You know how my mom get's when she wants something done. It's called taking command and running with it. You might as well surrender Unique. This battle is a done deal."

I shook my head in disbelief. "But what about what we..."

Mrs. Johnson was cleaning out her purse. "Where's my planner? Oh...here it is. As I was saying, I have taken the liberty to make us an appointment at the bridal boutique over there on the North Side. Then we have an appointment with the florist and the bakery on the South Side. Get your purse darling, we have to hurry."

"Mrs. Johnson, please you have to slow down. You still haven't told me where the wedding is going to take place. Don't you think we should have a say in one of the biggest days of our lives?"

Mrs. Johnson patted my hand. "Oh, I'm sorry, dear. Well, the church is out for two reasons, number one being Pastor's unavailability and secondly you're showing. You couldn't possibly walk down a church aisle. What would the congregation say? Anyway, Grant and I decided that our backyard is spacious enough to hold a simple but elegant and quaint wedding. You can get married under the gazebo. We will decorate it with some ribbons and flowers. It will look marvelous. You don't have to worry your pretty little head about a thing. Big Momma and I are in control. We have planned many parties and events for the upper crust of society when Justin was a judge. Oh…before I forget Grant's Uncle Marshall is a professional photographer and he's agreed to take your wedding pictures at no charge. It's his gift to you and Grant. You see my dear Unique; most of the work is halfway done."

My head was about to explode. Maybe, I was being hormonal but this was going too far. I didn't know if I should be happy or if I wanted to knock Mrs. Johnson right on out. She had some nerve coming to my house and dictating to me how my weeding was supposed to be. Ugh! I was beyond pissed and Grant knew it too.

"Grant, can I speak to you upstairs alone…please? Mrs. Johnson, please feel free to make yourself at home."

"Unique, there is no need to run upstairs. Grant agrees with me. Besides I'm leaving. Be in my driveway in ten minutes. We have lots to do!"

Mrs. Johnson grabbed her purse and planner from the sofa and marched out the house leaving us bewildered.

"Grant, do you really want to do this marriage thing now? Are you comfortable with your mother taking over our lives like this? She's like an uncontrollable hurricane. I've never seen her so hyper."

"Unique, come here and sit down beside me. Look, I really don't agree with my mother taking over everything. But Unique, she is so happy. This is the first time in months that I have seen her smile so much. Would it really hurt us to give her some happiness? Besides, we are living in sin and I don't want our baby to be born into a house full of negativity. The best gift we can give our child is for us to be married when he or she is born. So can you please just let my mother and Big Momma have their way just this once? I promise you we will live our own lives and make our own decisions."

Grant planted a warm and tender kiss on my lips. He got me every time.

"Okay Grant, if it will make you happy, then I'm happy. I say let's get this party started. I better go call Ruby and Char. They are going to flip. I need them as bridesmaids. I hope they can get some inexpensive tickets to come home. Oh…my God…there are just so many things to do in a week's time. Our wedding day will be here before we know it."

"Unique, Momma is outside blowing her horn. You better save your calls until you get back. I have to work tonight. I'm going to take a nap. I'll make sure I lock up when I leave. Don't wait up for me. Try to have some fun and don't get stressed out. Stress isn't good for you or the baby. See you later my love."

"I'll try not to panic. I realize your mom is just trying to be a sweetheart. I…I just miss my Momma. She should be here helping me plan the biggest day of my life."

Grant walked me over toward the front door then wrapped his arms around my expanding waistline and engulfed me with a tight hug as I collapsed into his chest allowing a few tears to escape from my eyes.

"Unique, I know you miss your mother. I wish I could bring her back for you. But remember she is always in your heart and soul. I know she is in heaven watching over you. Now scat before the neighbors call the police on my mother. She has been honking for the past three minutes."

"Bye, Grant. I love you."

"Bye, Sunshine. I love you too. Have fun."

Mrs. Johnson and I literally shopped until we dropped. I tried on five gowns before I went back and purchased the first dress I had picked out. Mrs. Johnson cried the entire time. She said they were tears of joy. I didn't really believe her but there was nothing I could do to make her stop.

I didn't buy a white wedding gown because I felt like a big fat marshmallow. Instead, I opted for a champagne colored raw silk gown. The dress was incredible and it screamed elegance. It made me feel like a beautiful princess. I looked absolutely stunning. It had a square neck which dipped low enough to show off a tasteful amount of cleavage. It was also off the shoulders and very form fitting until it got to my waist then it bellowed out. My pregnancy was hardly visible. The back of the dress was completely out and it narrowed into a "v" shape at the bottom, right before my buttocks. That was where a beautiful bow was placed and around the edges beautiful pearls and sequences accented the gown. The train was exquisite.

I found the perfect veil with a tiny diamond Tierra attached to it. My strapless champagne colored shoes were also adorned with pearls and sequences. They were so comfortable I knew I could dance all night at our reception.

When we left the bridal shop Mrs. Johnson and I went to the florist. My bouquet consisted of my favorite flowers the Stargazer

Lilies. The lilies were accentuated with a few babies' breath and pink roses. I loved the mock version the florist quickly assembled. We also ordered an assortment of pink flowers for Ruby and Char to carry as well. Three pink roses were ordered to serve as boutonnières for Grant and his two groomsmen.

After we spent an hour at the florist, we went to Smith's Bakery in Wilkinsburg and ordered the cake. Mrs. Johnson paid for everything. I offered to reimburse her but she wouldn't hear of it. She said my money was our nest egg and we should keep it for a rainy day.

It was close to nine in the evening before Mrs. Johnson pulled up to my house. She took my gorgeous dress home with her. We both knew Grant was so nosey he would be unable to keep his hands off of the dress if it remained at my house.

I was completely exhausted. I had no idea Mrs. Johnson could run the streets like that. For a middle aged woman she had a lot of spunk. As I ran into the house I felt like I had been hit head on by a freight train. By the time I took my shower, ate and got settled I had finally mustered up some extra energy to contact Ruby and Char. Oh…man, it's close to midnight were did the time go? They are probably out at the club. I'm just going to take a chance and pray they are home. I can't wait for tomorrow. I enthusiastically dialed Ruby's number.

"Hello, Ruby?"

"No, this is Rita. I'm Ruby's roommate. Who's calling?"

"Hi, Rita, this is Unique."

"Um…who?"

"My name is Unique…Unique Blackman. I'm a friend of Ruby's. Is she available?"

"Hold on I'll get her."

"Thanks."

"You are welcome. Ru…beeee…phone. It's some girl named Um…U… What's your name again?"

"It's Unique!"

"Yeah, that's right. Ru…beeee it's Unique."

"Unique girl, how have you been? Your ears must have been burning because Char and I were just talking about you. We are going to a frat party. Unique, you should see the brothers that go to Morehouse; they make you weak in the knees. Every man I have met is finer than the next. I tell you at least fifty percent of the brothers are finer than Grant. By the way, how is the daddy to be?"

"Grant is wonderful but you know that already. That's why you are trying your hardest to find a man like him."

"Girl, you know that's right. You never lie."

"What's up with your roommate Ree…ta? She's special."

"Rita is cool people."

"She may be cool but she couldn't get my name together. You know how that irritates me."

"Forget about her. Tell me why you called? Time is clicking, away Miss Blackman."

"I have great news to share with you and Char. Can you do a three way with Char? I want to tell you two together."

"Oh, this must be really big news. Hold on. She might have left for the party already."

"Hello."

"Char, is that you?"

"Yeah, it's me Ruby. I was just ready to walk out the door. What do you want? We should have been at the party fifteen minutes ago."

"Char, Unique's on the line. She has something to tell us."

"What's up, Unique? How's that bun in the oven?"

"I'm fine, Char. In fact, I'm better than fine. Grant and I are getting married next Saturday."

"What?" The girls said in unison.

"Ruby did you hear Unique?"

"Yeah, I heard her Char. Ha…ha Unique. You're really funny. Do you mind repeating yourself? I think we have a bad connection."

"You heard me. Grant and I are getting married next Saturday. I have been out shopping all day with Mrs. Johnson. I just walked in the door. I have my dress, shoes, stockings and veil. I ordered the flowers and the cake. There really isn't that much left to do."

"And where are these nuptials taking place? I can't believe you were able to get a church and reception hall so fast. When my sister Chandra got married last year, she had to book a church and a reception hall a year in advance."

"You're right, Char. My brother Russell is getting married next year and they are looking at places now."

"Ruby, we aren't getting married in a church."

Ruby and Char shouted at me, "What!"

"The ceremony is going to take place in the Johnson's backyard under the gazebo. A Judge, who is a good friend of Mrs. Johnson will officiate the service."

"But what about, Pastor? I always thought you wanted a church wedding."

"I did Char, but Pastor is out of town. And the more I think about it I would feel very uncomfortable walking down the aisle in a church with a baby on board. I also called you because I want you two to be my bridesmaids. I know its short notice. Can you get away? I'll understand if you can't make it."

"Girl, when you do something, you don't waste a moment. What are Char and I supposed to wear?"

"Yeah, girl. I know my parents won't give me any money for a dress. They just sent the school a great big check."

"It's okay, ladies. I've got you covered. I thought since it is the end of September you could get away with wearing your prom dresses. It's going to be an afternoon wedding so I'm praying for another warm day. So are you two in or out?"

An ecstatic Ruby spoke, "I'm in. I wouldn't miss your wedding for anything."

An excited Char screamed, "Count me in too." Since you have given us such short notice, it will be expensive to buy plane tickets at this late date. They will cost an arm and a leg."

"Oh…Char I didn't think about that. I can buy your tickets for both of you. It will be my treat."

"Girl, please. You are about to start a family, so you better hold on to your inheritance. I have my car and I like to drive. I'll just pick up Ruby after our last class on Friday. My last class is at one. Ruby what time is your class over?"

"Char, you know I have the best schedule. I have one class on Friday and that's over at ten."

"Ruby, I knew there was a reason why I can't stand you."

"I love you to Miss Char."

"Unique, we will probably get on the road by two since some of us are taking more classes than required. I've never driven from Atlanta to Pittsburgh so I'm going to estimate and say we should be at your house by midnight or later."

"Char, you are tripping it won't take us eight hours unless you are driving as slow as a turtle."

"Okay, Ruby then you tell us how long it takes? I don't remember you ever driving to Pittsburgh or anywhere else. Maybe it's because you don't have a car."

"Char, you're such a comedian. You're right I don't have the slightest idea. But, I know one thing you drive way too slow! I could probably walk to Pittsburgh and get there hours before you."

"Fine then Ruby go ahead and walk. I hope you have some good soles on your shoes."

"Char, there you go again with those jokes."

"I see nothing has changed between you two. I miss you guys so much. I can't wait to see you."

"Look Unique, I love and miss you too but there are some fine Negroes waiting for me over at Morehouse. Now we are thirty minutes late. I really need to jump off of this phone. Momma's got to get her a brand new man. Watch out now."

"A new man? Char, what happened to Derek?"

"Girl, that will take an hour to explain and at this point I don't have to an hour to spare. I'll catch you Friday. Ruby, meet me in the lobby in two minutes. Love you, Unique."

"Love you Char. Love you Ruby."

"We love you too, Unique. Damn, can we please get off the phone? We ain't the Waltons." Char chuckled.

I hung up from my best friends with a feeling that the rest of my life was going to be wonderful. I couldn't wait for Saturday.

Chapter 13

At last my dream was coming true. I was about to become Mrs. Grant Montgomery Johnson. I was so nervous I could hardly contain my excitement. I guess our baby girl was ecstatic too because this morning was the first day I felt her kick. Yes indeed, this is going to be a lovely day.

I know this would probably sound very ridiculous but I swear I felt my Momma's presence. At one point, I even thought I smelled her perfume. I must be hallucinating.

Char and Ruby arrived at my house late Friday night. They decided to stay the night instead of going home. They wanted to make sure I got up early enough to get prepared for my big day. I was always hungry so we ordered from Mineo's, two large pepperoni pizzas with mushrooms and two bottles of the two-liter size of Pepsi. We reminisced and talked into the wee hours of the morning. We remembered all the crazy things we did in elementary, middle, and high school. We really had some great times together. The years passed us by so quickly.

The last thing I remembered talking to Char and Ruby was the time we were in eleventh grade and we decided to skip school. We drove to Ohio so we could go to Cedar Point. We got busted because the car broke down on the way home. It was after midnight when we finally called our parents and asked for someone to pick us up on the Turnpike at the Youngstown exit. By the time, we called our parents, they were hysterical. They just knew someone had kidnapped us. That stunt caused us our last whipping and punishment. Char's mom even took her car keys away. The final blow was when we were told we could not hang out after school and our phone privileges were revoked. We spent an entire month in agony.

I was the first one to drift off to sleep. The next thing I knew Char and Ruby were standing over me.

"Rise and shine, Miss Sleepyhead. It's your wedding day." Char said as she jumped up and down on my bed.

I moaned, "Five more minutes. Please, just five more minutes."

"Get up girl! We have lots of work to do. You know you need a complete makeover. Now get up!" Ruby screamed at the top of her lungs as she hit me in the head with a pillow. Then she joined

Char as they continued to jump up and down on the bed as hard as they could until they bounced me right out and onto the floor. Char and Ruby collapsed on the bed as they laughed their butts off. I laid on the floor laughing until my stomach started to ache.

That moment reminded me of the many joyous sleepovers Char, Ruby, and I shared. I was always the first one to fall asleep. The next morning, Char and Ruby bounced me out of the bed. I was so thrilled to share this special day with my girls. I didn't know what I would have done without them. It was hard to believe after all of these years they still have my best interest at heart. I guess we would be this way until our dying day.

I looked out my bedroom window to find the sun shinning brightly. For once, the forecaster was right in predicting the weather. The temperature would reach an unusual high of eighty degrees. It looked like Indian summer came right in the nick of time.

Char put my hair up in a French roll, leaving some hair out so it could be swooped into a dangling bang on the right side of my face. Ruby applied my makeup and then placed the Tierra and veil on top of my head.

For my something old, I wore my mother's diamond earrings and tennis bracelet. The delicate handkerchief that went in my garter was purchased by Ruby. It served as my something blue and my something new. Char let me borrow her pearl necklace. I slipped on a pair of jeans, and tennis shoes. I grabbed my wedding shoes off of my bed, locked up the house, and we were on our way up to the Johnsons household.

When we arrived at the Johnson home, we saw Mrs. Johnson peering out the living room window. She was eagerly awaiting our arrival. Mrs. Johnson quickly ushered us upstairs to the master bedroom so I could put on my dress. This was the first time in a long time I saw Mrs. Johnson's eyes twinkle. She was overjoyed.

"My dear Unique, you look absolutely breathtaking and you don't even have your dress on yet. Grant is going to be overcome with delight when he sees you walking down the aisle."

"Thank you so much, Mrs. Johnson. Thanks for everything."

"You're welcome, my dear. Unique, I am telling you, you look so radiant. What salon did you go to this morning? Your hair and makeup is simply wonderful. Your skin is flawless not a pimple insight."

"Mrs. Johnson, I didn't go to any salon. Ruby did my makeup and Char fixed my hair."

Mrs. Johnson turned toward my girls and showed her award winning smile and said "Girls, you outdid yourselves."

Char and Ruby responded with even bigger smiles which spread across their faces. "Thank you, Mrs. Johnson."

"You're welcome. If I knew you two had such hidden talents, I would have let you do something with this mop of mine. Oh…well. Unique, dear can you please do something for me?"

"Sure, Mrs. Johnson, I'll do anything for you. Just name it."

"You know I have watched you blossom from a sweet little girl into a wonderful, mature, sensitive, young woman. I am so proud of you. I feel like you are my daughter so…I…I…what I am trying to get at is…I was wondering do you think that you could call me Mom? I know I can't take the place of your mother…"

I fought back the tears. "Mrs. Johnson, no one can take the place of my mother but you have always supported and loved me. I have always thought of you in that way. It would be an honor to officially call you Mom."

"Oh…Unique, you have made me extremely happy."

Char and Ruby were already crying. "This is a Kodak moment," said Ruby threw her tears. Mrs. Johnson was holding me so tight she got a big surprise.

"My God, Unique, was that the baby kicking me?"

"I believe your grandchild is happy too, Mom."

"Lord…Lord…Lord. Hallelujah." I thought Mrs. Johnson was going to have a massive coronary. She yelled so loud Big Momma came running in.

"Ingrid, what in God's name is going on in here? Why are you yelling like the house is on fire?"

"Momma, hurry up and come here. Quick, feel Unique's stomach. Your great grandchild is kicking up a storm."

Big Momma, who was standing in the bedroom doorway, peered at us and walked slowly toward my belly. She placed her hand on my stomach right as the baby gave another hard kick. "My, my, my…looks like we got a football player in the family. That's a kick of a big ole boy."

"Aw…Big Momma, I want a girl."

"Sorry, Angel, I hate to disappoint you but what you got brewing in that belly is a strong and healthy baby boy. Believe me, I have been on this here earth a mighty long time and I've never been wrong in predicting the sex of a baby."

"Unique!" shouted Char, "It's almost three. We need to get you in your dress."

Mrs. Johnson looked at her watch to confirm the time. "My goodness, time has flown by so quickly. Are you ready Unique?"

"Yes, Mom, I'm so ready."

"Good dear. Well, Big Momma and I are going to tend to the guests and get the ceremony under way. You girls speed things up and get Unique ready, quick fast and in a hurry. I can't stand it when black folk's weddings start thirty minutes to an hour late. It throws the word, etiquette, right out the door."

Ruby and Char acknowledged Mrs. Johnson. "Yes, Mrs. Johnson. We will have her ready in five minutes."

"Actually, girls you've got two minutes, and Unique..."

"Yes?"

"I love you. I am so pleased you are now officially apart of our family."

I was really emotional. I tried very hard to choke back my tears but they flowed like a river. "I love you too."

With nothing else, left to be said Mrs. Johnson and Big Momma smiled and walked out the room.

"Look at you, Unique. Now I have to fix your makeup. You look like a raccoon."

"Sorry, Ruby."

Before I knew it, Char, Ruby and I were descending down the steps. We walked thru the living room, past the kitchen, and into the family room that led us toward the backyard.

My breath was taken away as I looked outside to see the beautifully decorated gazebo. Mrs. Johnson even had the guest chairs decorated with gorgeous flowers and ribbons. I had no idea the backyard would look so breathtaking. I was truly amazed.

The triplets who were now six years old were in the wedding too. Like their big brother Grant, Malcolm and Marvin were dressed in black tuxes with tails. They looked so adorable. Malcolm carried the pillow with the rings on it while Marvin followed closely behind him carrying the broom for us to jump over after we are pronounced man and wife.

Now, little Miss Marra almost stole the show. She was dressed in a white-laced dress. The dress was accented by a flowing pink ribbon, which tied around her waist into a big bow. Her hair was full of Shirley Temple curls that bounced all of her head with each step she took. She was absolutely the prettiest little girl I had ever seen. Marra preceded me down the aisle while she dropped pink and white rose petals.

I felt as if I were in a dream as I floated down the aisle while listening to the harpist play the "Wedding March." Grant was devastatingly handsome in his tux. He stood next to his two beaming college buddies who served as groomsmen.

As I approached the gazebo, I kept my gaze transfixed on Grant. I was hypnotized by his magnetic grin that was spread across his face. I almost fainted when I saw him casually wiping a tear from his eye.

I stole a quick look at Ruby and Char as they were passing tissues to each other. Big Momma and Mrs. Johnson cried too as they held on to each other. Meanwhile, Uncle Marshall was busily snapping pictures. The bright flash from his camera blinded me momentarily.

As the "Wedding March" faded into the distance, I took my place next to Grant.

Judge Houston asked, "Who gives this bride away?" Mrs. Johnson, Big Momma, Char, and Ruby yelled, "We do." I was pleasantly surprised.

I was so edgy my heart felt as if it were beating in my throat. I didn't think I could stand a moment longer as my legs began to sway. Grant reached out, gently took my hand, and moved me closer to him. His touch was electrifying. I was overcome with a rush of adrenaline. Grant leaned into me and whispered in my ear, "You look incredible."

At that moment, any apprehension I felt about our marriage or our baby melted away as quickly as ice melts to a flame. I knew then the purity of our love was solid and everlasting. There was no doubt in my mind our love would stand the test of time. By three thirty, Grant and I were pronounced husband and wife.

Uncle Marshall went overboard with his photography duties. If he asked me to smile one more time for the camera, I was going to scream. My face felt as if it were cracking from smiling so much.

After the ceremony, Mrs. Johnson and Big Momma went into the house to make sure the caterers were ready to serve the food to our guests.

****

"Momma, wasn't the ceremony just wonderful?"

"Child, it sure was. I never thought I would see my first grandchild married at such a young age. Grant made a mistake by knocking Unique up but I'm proud of him. He stepped up to the plate and became a man. He's doing the right thing. It's going to be hard on them two cause they just babies themselves trying to be grown. But I've prayed and the good Lord will watch over them. You know God takes care of fools and babies. Yes, indeed they are going to be just fine."

"Momma, I miss Justin so much that sometimes I just want to scream and yell at God, why…why did you do this to me?"

"Baby, God knows your pain and there is a reason for everything. Sometimes it takes us a while to get the revelation of God's plan. You must remember God makes no mistakes."

"Momma, I know, He doesn't. It's just so sad. Justin should have been here for his son's wedding. I know deep down inside he would be proud of the man Grant has become. I believe he would have adjusted to Unique being his daughter in-law once he laid eyes on that baby. But…that will never happen. Momma, when did your heart stop aching for Daddy?"

"Ingrid, it's been over twenty-five years since we buried my sweet, sweet Henry. Not a day goes by I don't think about him. I miss his strong arms, his wonderful smile and silly jokes. Henry was a prankster, a good man and an excellent provider. He was a hard worker who loved and took care of his family. His most important quality was he loved the Lord. I don't reckon you truly ever get over the pain it just subsides somewhat but it still lingers deep down in the bottom of your soul. Give it time, baby. The cut is still fresh and opened. They say time heals all wounds."

"Are you healed, Momma?"

"Hmm…well…I don't reckon I will ever be completely healed. Don't think I want to because that would mean I have forgotten about my Henry. Some days my memories are the only thing that keeps me going. You know God doesn't give us more than we can bear. No… I reckon I'm not healed."

"Momma, I'm so blessed to have you in my life. I don't know what I would do if I lost you. You have been my support and my rock. I love you, Momma."

"Ingrid, you know Momma loves you too. Now fetch me some punch. I'm going on over to my favorite chair and sit down. I need to take a load off of my swollen feet. I'm not as young as I used to be. This ole gal is a little sleepy. The wedding has gotten me all off schedule. It's way past my nap time."

"Momma, let me help you get in the chair."

"Girl, I ain't too decrepit that I need someone to help me sit down. I'll be just fine."

"Okay, Momma. Hey, after dinner, would you like some wedding cake?"

"Ingrid, now you know I got a little "sugar". But I suppose a little sliver wouldn't hurt."

"Momma, there's no such thing as a little "sugar". Diabetes is diabetes. So I'll tell you how the cake tastes."

"Ingrid, why did you ask me if you weren't going to give me any?"

"Oh, I was just testing you Momma. By the way, Miss Gertrude called me early this morning."

"What? What did that ole busy body want? You know she never has a nice thing to say about anyone."

"Momma, Miss Gertrude is concerned about you and your health."

"Now that's a joke. Gertrude ain't ever been concerned about anyone but herself. This should be real interesting. What did the ole crow say?"

"She said that you had two large slices of sweet potato pie last night at your bingo game. She also said you checked your blood later and it was way over two hundred."

"That ole bitty. She has been telling on me all her life. With friends like her, I truly don't need any enemies. I'm going to call her when I get home and give her a piece of my mind. She got some nerve calling you and telling all my business. You ain't my momma. The ole b…"

"Momma! You know that Miss Gertrude is just looking out for you."

"I bet she is. Why don't you call Gertrude and ask her why she isn't here? I'll tell you why, she still got a hangover, the old geezer. Girl, just go and get me some punch. All this talking has made me even thirstier. And turn up the air. I'm sweating up a storm in here. That Gertrude I tell you is a spear in my side."

"Okay, Momma, don't get your blood pressure up. I'll get your punch. I'll be right back."

"Thanks darling."

"You're welcome."

****

Mrs. Johnson went outside and walked toward the table that held the punch bowel and cups when she was distracted by the beautiful music that serenaded the guests. The harpist was playing "You and I" by Stevie Wonder as Grant and I danced our first dance as husband and wife. A tear left Mrs. Johnson's eye as she thought about her wedding with Justin.

Grant and I were oblivious to our surroundings. Our eyes were locked in each other's gaze. We were deeply captivated with each other's love. Our hearts beat as one. Our embrace was abruptly broken when we heard a heart-wrenching scream that came from the direction of the family room.

"Lord, no! No…not again! Oh…sweet Jesus. Lord have mercy!"

Grant and I, along with our guests, made a mad dash to the family room where we found Mrs. Johnson kneeling in front of Big Momma. A broken glass of punch was on the floor.

Big Momma was sitting in the corner of the family room in her favorite brown leather chair. Her feet were propped on the ottoman and her head was leaning forward as if she were praying.

"Momma! What's wrong?" Grant shouted.

Mrs. Johnson kept repeating, "No…no…no…not my Momma Lord. Not my sweet, sweet Momma."

Grant tried to pull his mother away from Big Momma but she held on to her for dear life. That was when Grant lifted Big Momma's head up only to see her head and body slump forward onto Mrs. Johnson.

Chaos broke out as the guests screamed in horror. I was hysterically crying and shouting at anyone and everyone, "Get an ambulance!"

Within ten minutes, the paramedics arrived at the house. They tried to resuscitate her but it was too late. Big Momma died from an apparent heart attack.

Mrs. Johnson was extremely devastated. She was so distraught she had to be given a tranquilizer. What started out as the most beautiful day of my life ended as one of the worst days of my life. I hope this wasn't an omen of what our future would become. I wondered if our life would be forever marred by today's events.

Chapter 13

Christmas just wouldn't be Christmas without Big Momma. It was her favorite time of the year. She loved the hustle and bustle the season would bring. She almost became child-like when she shopped with Mrs. Johnson. Then she would stay up half the night wrapping each present beautifully as if it were on display at a department store.

Our family had endured tremendous losses during the year of 1976, with the death of Daddy, Mr. Johnson, and now Big Momma. I knew 1977 had to be a better year. Yes, it was going to be better because a new life, our child was going to be born.

Mrs. Johnson was in some sort of deep depression. She barely came to the house for a visit. Most nights, the triplets stayed with us. On several occasions after work, I had to pick the triplets up and cook them dinner. After work, Mrs. Johnson went straight home and got in the bed. Her strange behavior extended into the weekends. Sleep was her new best friend. She took off from work so much she used all of her sick days and was now working on her vacation days.

When she decided to go to work, she ignored her coworkers. In her twenty year career at the bank, Mrs. Johnson was a model employee. Mrs. Johnson had an impeccable record. Her evaluations were always superb. But now her supervisor was giving her a bad performance appraisal. Mrs. Johnson had become trapped within herself. She was just going through the daily motions of every day life. Her heart just wasn't in anything anymore. Just when you think things can't get any worse, they somehow do.

December 24, 1976 was another horrific day. Grant came running in the house. "Unique! Unique!"

"I'm upstairs in the bathtub. What's wrong?"

Grant rushed into the bathroom with my robe. "Get out of the tub. Hurry up."

"Grant, what in the world is wrong with you?"

"Damn it! Unique, just do it!"

"What?"

"I'm sorry, baby. Please dry off and put on your robe and slippers. I need you to come outside with me."

"Outside?"

"Yes, outside. Hurry."

I jumped out of the tub, quickly dried off and ran downstairs with Grant. He opened up the front door as a cold harsh wind ripped right through my robe, sending chills up my spine. We stepped out of the doorway and onto the front porch.

"Grant it's freezing out here. What do you want me to see?"

"Unique, look up the street to Mom's house and tell me what do you see posted in the front lawn?"

"Oh…my…it's a for sale sign. Grant it must be a mistake. Your mother wouldn't think about moving without telling us."

"Unique, I watched the realtor hammer the sign into the ground. Then Momma came out of the house and shook the realtor's hand. I never thought I would see this day. I don't know what I should do."

"What we are going to do is go up there and find out what is really going on. Come back inside while I put on my clothes. Don't worry, Grant. There has to be a reasonable explanation. Maybe your mom wanted to move into that new development. She did receive a nice inheritance from your father and Big Momma.

"Maybe, you're right Unique, but…that…that was Momma and Daddy's first house they purchased together. I can't imagine Momma would want to leave all those memories. We had some really good times in that house."

"Perhaps, Grant, the issue is there are too many memories existing in the house. Maybe they are too much for your mother to handle. She hasn't been in the right state of mind for awhile now."

Grant hung his head low and said in a barely audible mumble, "I know. Nothing is like it used to be."

I left Grant for a few moments while I ran upstairs to our bedroom to put on some warm clothes. When I came back downstairs, Grant was sitting on the couch crying. I sat down beside him and gently pulled him to my breast. I held him tight as he released all of his emotions. "It's going to be alright honey. I promise you, it's going to be alright." I rocked him until the sobs subsided.

About fifteen minutes later, we arrived at Mrs. Johnson's house but she would not answer the door. We could hear the triplets screaming, "Momma, someone's at the door." Grant decided to use his key.

The triplets jumped on us as soon as we opened the door. We gave them lots of hugs and kisses. They were starving for attention.

Grant asked Malcolm, "Where is Mommy?"

"She's in the family room staring at the TV."

Grant and I looked at the sad children. I spoke to the triplets. "You kids go on upstairs and get ready for bed. I'll come up and read you a story. I heard Santa left the North Pole and he is on his way."

"Yippee! Unique is going to read us a stor…ree." They chanted as they zoomed off to their bedrooms.

"And brush your teeth." Grant hollered behind them.

"Come on, Grant. We need to check on your mother."

"I'm right behind you."

Grant and I approached the darkened family room. The illumination from the television set was the only light on in the room. Grant turned on a lamp and turned off the TV. Mrs. Johnson did not move a muscle.

"Momma, tell me you are not selling the house?"

"I saw you looking at me when the realtor came by to put the sign up. I'm surprised it took you so long to come up here. Where are the kids?"

"Mom, the kids are getting ready for bed. Would you like me to make you some hot chocolate?"

"That would be nice, Unique. Grant, you keep her, you hear me?"

"Grant, do you want a cup?"

"No, thanks, I'm fine. Momma, why are you selling the house?"

"Lower your voice, boy! You are never going to be old enough to disrespect me."

"Momma, I apologize. Could you please tell me what is going on?"

"Do you remember my Delta sorority sister, Emily?"

"I vaguely remember. Why?"

"Well, she called me the other day to wish me a Merry Christmas. She just got back from Europe. Anyway, I told her life wasn't very merry anymore. I told her you were married now and my dear, dear husband and sweet momma were dead. We talked for a long time. I think it was for a couple of hours at least."

"Here, Mom. Your hot chocolate is ready. Be careful the cup is awfully hot."

"Thank you, Unique. You keep her boy. Don't let anyone or anything come between you."

"Momma, I have no plans of getting rid of Unique. I love her. You know that. I promise you right here, right now you don't have to worry about us. Please Momma, you still haven't told me why you are selling this house? What does this Emily person have to do with anything?"

"Boy, you never had much patience. I'm trying to find the right words to tell you. Emily is some type of government auditor so they want her to go back to Europe and live there for another year. She told me I need a change of scenery and the kids and I should come out to visit before she leaves. Well, one thing led to another and I decided me and the kids are going to house-sit."

"Momma, this doesn't make any sense. You don't have to sell this house if you are just going to watch someone's house. Unique and I can water your plants and take care of things. I'll even paint the entire house for you, so when you and the kids get back it will be nice and fresh. It will look brand new. I can even lay the new carpet you were looking at awhile back."

"Son, that won't be necessary."

"Momma, please whatever you want done… I'll do it."

"Grant, listen to me, we aren't coming back."

"I don't believe you, Momma."

"Mom, where does Miss Emily live?"

"She lives in Florida."

Grant and I shout "Florida?"

"Get the wax out your ears. Florida is what I said. We are moving the first of the year."

"But Mom you are going to miss the birth of your granddaughter."

"Unique darling, Big Momma told you, you were having a boy. She's never been wrong."

"Momma, I just don't understand. You haven't seen Miss Emily in how long? How do you know if you will even like Florida? How could you leave us? How could you take the kids? I've already lost so much."

"Hush now, son. You have Unique and this baby. They are all the family you need."

Grant rushed into his mother arms and sobbed. "Momma, I'll always need you."

Mrs. Johnson rubbed his head. "You'll be just fine child. Just fine."

"Unique, Unique, come read us a story." The triplets yelled from the top of the stairs.

"I'm coming."

Grant and Mrs. Johnson were so involved in their embrace they didn't notice me when I left the room. I think they needed some time to themselves anyway.

I read three stories to the triplets and then I tucked them into bed. After they said their prayers, I kissed them good night, turned off the lights, and started to walk downstairs when I heard Marra screaming to her brothers, "I see Rudolph! His nose is blinking in the sky." I laughed and said, "Well, you better go to sleep quickly or Santa might leave you a bunch of coal." I didn't hear another peep.

I walked back into the family room to find Grant and his mother holding hands.

"Grant you go on home. It's getting late. Unique needs her rest. Tomorrow is another day. You still have me around for another week."

"Okay, Momma. We will be up here early so we can open the presents. I'll even cook you a nice breakfast."

"That would be nice son. Good night. Make sure you turn the alarm on when you leave."

"I will. You get some rest Momma. Maybe you will be thinking clearer in the morning."

"No need to think clearer Grant, my mind is made up and you can't change it. I love you."

"I love you too." Grant said between his choking tears.

"Good night Mom. Love you."

"Good night my dear. You take care of my son."

"I always will for all eternity. You don't have to worry about that."

"You two are going to have a wonderful life. Now scat."

Grant and I turned on the alarm, locked up the house, and walked home in silence. I couldn't find the right words to console my husband's aching heart. At this point, all I could do was to be there for him when he was ready to talk.

In spite of the turmoil in our life, it was a wondrous and magnificent night. The brilliant moon was full and glowed in the dark sky. A crisp breeze filled the air and the wind howled ever so lightly. Huge snowflakes sparkled like diamonds as they descended quickly from the heavens leaving a thick coating on the ground and trees.

When we arrived at our house, Grant went inside as I stayed behind for a moment. I stood on our front porch and stood in awe of the beauty God had created. I looked up toward the sky and watched the twinkling stars that shone brightly threw the snow. I said a prayer for Mom and Grant because they needed the one present I couldn't give them. They needed a miracle.

Chapter 14

February roared in bringing more snow and colder temperatures. Schools were closed and many businesses did not open because of the fury of Mother Nature. Blizzards and a dropping wind chill factor made it unbearable to be outside for any length of time.

Mrs. Johnson and the kids had now been gone for a month and a half. We hadn't heard from them either. Grant was beside himself with worry. We called all the hospitals from here to Florida. Even the police were looking for our missing family.

While we were at work, Mrs. Johnson left us a message saying she and the kids arrived safely in Florida. She apologized for not calling sooner. She said she had to leave Pittsburgh because there were too many memories. She couldn't live in a house where her mother died. She also said everywhere she looked she saw reminders of Mr. Johnson. Before her message ended, Mrs. Johnson wished us love, peace, and happiness.

She left us no address or phone number. Mrs. Johnson and the kids just vanished from our lives. Grant was so devastated I thought he would never recover. But God always had a way of making things better.

At two in the morning on February 22, 1978, I went to the bathroom to relieve my full bladder. Before I could sit down on the cold porcelain seat, my water broke. I ran out of the room and frantically woke up Grant.

"Grant! Grant! Wake up! It's time."

"Time? It can't be time to go to work. I swear I just went to sleep. Besides, the alarm didn't ring. Sweetie, all I need is just another fifteen minutes."

"Grant! My water broke!"

"What?" Grant shouted as he jumped out of the bed. He grabbed his jeans and threw on a sweatshirt. He was dressed in a minute flat, while I struggled to put on my clothes.

"Girl, just put on your robe we don't have time for you to get dressed. Let's go."

Grant helped me with my robe, carried me down the steps, and put me in the car.

He was about to drive off when I shouted, "Grant you forgot my suitcase."

"Dag gone it, Unique. Where is it?"

"Grant it's where you put it. It's on the left side of the bed."

"Oh…that's right. I remember. I'll be right back."

I chuckled between contractions as I watched my panic-stricken husband rush back inside the house. In thirty seconds, he was back in the car, throwing the suitcase in the backseat.

"Hold on, baby."

"Grant, slow down the roads are icy. I want to get to the hospital in one piece."

We arrived at the hospital in record time. What should have taken us forty minutes took us twenty. I know for sure Grant went through four stop lights. I held my breath the entire time.

Grant drove up to the emergency entrance, jumped out of the car, ran inside, got a nurse, and a wheelchair. In no time, I was whisked away into the hospital.

Grant stayed behind to fill out all the necessary paperwork as I went to the delivery room to get prepped.

Fifteen minutes later, Grant was in the delivery room holding my hand. I had a really bad contraction.

"Unique baby, you are crushing my hand. I never knew you were so strong. Breathe baby breathe, that's it you are doing great."

Dr. Sampson had to be called in because he was not working that night. He arrived about twenty minutes later. Dr. Sampson put on his surgical gown and gloves. He then proceeded to walk over to the delivery table. He lifted the white sheet that covered the lower half of my body and looked under it so he could see if the baby was coming.

"Mrs. Johnson, you are almost home, it won't be long now. I see your baby's head. Listen to me. At your next contraction, I want you to push nice and hard."

"Did you hear that Unique? He can see our baby's head."

"Oooouch! I can't do this. Oh…God help me. It hurts so badly."

"Push now, Mrs. Johnson. Again push. That's it one more time."

"I can't it hurts. The drugs aren't working. I need more drugs."

"Mrs. Johnson, I can't give you anything else it's too late."

"Damn it! I hurt!"

"I know sweetheart you're doing really good."

"Grant, don't tell me that again! Oh my Lord, here comes another one!"

"Push, Mrs. Johnson, push. Here comes the head. Push again. Here are the shoulders and…"

The next thing I heard was my baby crying. My God, the baby was here.

"Congratulations Mr. and Mrs. Johnson, you have a nine-pound two-ounce bouncing baby boy."

"A boy? A boy? Unique, did you hear that? We have a son."

I was crying uncontrollably. "Yes, Grant, I hear you. Big Momma was right. Doctor, can I hold him?"

"Just a minute, Mrs. Johnson, the nurse is cleaning him off and wrapping him in his blanket."

"I love you, Unique. Thank you for this blessing. We got ourselves a little man." Grant kissed me as the tears streamed down his face.

"Excuse me, Mr. and Mrs. Johnson. Someone wants to see their Mommy."

The nurse placed a beautiful baby in my arms. Grant and I looked him over from head to toe. He was perfect in every way. His head was fully covered with dark brown curly hair. He had ten little fingers and ten of the cutest chubby toes. Grant and I were astounded and in awe of the perfection of God's creation, His miracle that He bestowed to us. We just stared at him and watched as his lungs filled and exhaled with air. Underneath his blue blanket our baby boy wiggled and stretched ever so slightly as he turned and looked into my eyes. I loved him more than I ever could have imagined.

"Grant, do you want to hold your son?"

"Uh…I…I'm…nervous. It's been along time since I held a baby."

"He won't break. You won't hurt him. Here, take him." I placed our son in Grant's arms and he silently held him. Grant's face was full of pride and love for his new son. The tears released freely from our eyes as father and son got to know each other.

"Unique."

"Yes."

"Thank you. You went through so much while being pregnant but you managed to take care of yourself. Thank you from the bottom of my heart for giving me my son."

"Oh...Grant, I love you so very, very much."

"I love you too with every fiber of my being. I have never felt this type of love. It's indescribable."

"I know what you mean."

"Here Unique, take our son. You did all the hard work. He should be with his mother. Besides I think he wants to nurse. That definitely falls under the mommy duties."

Grant gently placed our son back in my arms. I held him and looked into his little eyes. I gently spoke to our son for the first time.

"Hi little fellow, I am your Mommy and this very handsome man is your Daddy. We have been anxiously awaiting your arrival. It's strange to have so much love for someone that you just met but I feel like I have loved you all of my life. Now your Daddy and I aren't perfect and we are going to make some mistakes along the way because you didn't arrive with instructions. But I can promise you that your Daddy and I will love, protect, and take care of you until our dying day. My prayer for you is God will bless you and keep you all the days of your life. Welcome to the world Clark Montgomery Johnson."

Chapter 15

On August 20, 1981, Shannell Alexandra Johnson made her entrance into the world screaming at the top of her lungs. She weighed six pounds and two ounces. Like her brother Clark, she had a head full of beautiful curly dark brown hair. She was a very delicate "girlie" looking baby.

Grant was a basket case around her. He thought she was too fragile to hold. Clark, on the other hand, loved his little sister and smothered her with kisses whenever he could.

Grant was in his third year of college and was still playing basketball. His hopes of going to the NBA were looking better and better with each passing day.

I was still at the bank but I had transferred to the Accounts Payable department. I needed a change and some more money. My trust fund seemed to be getting smaller and smaller with each passing year.

Our family was slowly out growing my daddy's house so we decided to sell it and move to Squirrel Hill.

With the equity in Daddy's house and the leftover money of my trust fund, we were able to move into a nice three thousand square foot home with five-bedrooms, four bathrooms, and a huge backyard for the kids.

When 1983 rolled around, we prepared for some major changes. In June Grant would be finished with college and he was in turmoil over the upcoming draft. We knew we might be moving but where was still a mystery.

Our life was more than we ever imagined. We had a wonderful home and two beautiful children. We were preparing to be taken to the next level. With the assurance of Grant turning pro, we could afford for me to stay home with the kids. I was really happy about that. Day care made me nervous. I wanted to raise my children. Grant's career as a professional basketball player would make us very comfortable.

Over the years, Grant had been on the cover of every college basketball and sports magazine. He was at the top of his game, which made him a strong contender as the first round draft pick for the NBA. Mr. Dickerson, his basketball coach, fondly called Grant the "Shooting Star" because of his height and the way he glided on the court when he was about to make a basket.

The future was looking very bright. However, one should never count their chickens before they hatch.

****

Grant was practicing with his team when Coach Dickerson asked Grant to dribble the ball down center court as his teammates tried to advance on him so they could take the ball from him. Grant and his team did this drill for a good twenty minutes. When Coach Dickerson was about to blow his whistle to start a new play Grant was rushed by two of his teammates. He was about to turn right when his teammate stepped on his foot. A loud crunch and pop was heard as Grant twisted his right knee. He landed on the basketball court with a big thud.

Grant screamed with excruciating pain as Coach Dickerson and the team doctors ran to his side. His teammates looked on in dismay as Grant hollered at the top of his lungs.

A worried Coach knelt next to Grant and held his hand. "Grant, son we're here to help you."

Riddled with pain Grant spoke. "My knee, Coach, it feels like it has been ripped off. Can you give me something for the pain?"

"Hold on, son. Doc Bell is right here. Doc, please do something for the boy. Look at him. He's losing his color because he's hurting so bad. Move back boys so the doctors can do their job."

****

I was at home giving Shannell and Clark a bath when the phone rang. I hurriedly took the children out of the tub so I could run to the bedroom and answer the call.

"Hello."

"Is this Mrs. Unique Johnson?"

"Yes, this is Mrs. Johnson. May I help you?"

"Mrs. Johnson, this is Coach Dickerson."

"Coach Dickerson, it is so nice to hear from you. Is practice over already?"

"Mrs. Johnson, practice was cut short this evening."

"Oh…okay. Did Grant leave something behind after practice? Is that why you are calling? Knowing Grant, he was probably in a rush to get home. He's good for leaving something behind."

"Mrs. Johnson, Grant didn't leave anything. I'm afraid that this isn't a social call. I'm calling because I have some bad news concerning Grant."

"Bad news? Concerning Grant? …What! What is it? What's wrong with my husband?"

"Well, there was an accident on the court."

"What sort of accident? What could possibly happen to him at practice?"

"Mrs. Johnson, please calm down."

"How can I be calm when you are telling me that something has happened to my Grant? Where is he? I want to speak with him."

"I'm sorry Mrs. Johnson but you can't speak to him. Grant has been rushed to Shadyside Hospital. We need you to get there right away. It looks like he might have to have surgery."

"Surgery?"

"Mrs. Johnson, from what our team doctors have told me, Grant apparently tore his ligaments and tendons in his knee cap. We aren't one hundred percent positive but I can tell you he's in a lot of pain."

"I'm on my way. I just have to dress my children. What about…never mind."

"Mrs. Johnson, the doctors will be able to tell us more once he is x-rayed. I don't know if Grant's career is over, but you don't worry about that now. I'll meet you at the emergency entrance."

"Goodbye, Coach."

"See you soon, Mrs. Johnson."

I sat on the bed momentarily to gather my thoughts as Clark and Shannell climbed all over me. Grant was going to be devastated if he could not play ball anymore. My God, how am I supposed to deal with that?

In less than an hour, I arrived at the hospital emergency room. Coach Dickerson was waiting for me.

"Mrs. Johnson?"

"Please call me, Unique. Where is my husband?"

"The doctors took him to x-ray. They should be back shortly. And who are these beautiful children?"

"Clark, say hello to the Coach."

Clark just looked at the Coach, as a sleepy Shannell lay in my arms.

"Shy, are we son? Would you like a piece of candy?"

Clark looked up at me awaiting my approval.

"It's okay Clark, you can have one piece. Say thank you."

A faint "Thank you" escaped Clark's mouth. The Coach patted him on the head and gave him the candy.

An elderly doctor, who walked with a slight limp in his left leg, entered the waiting area of the emergency room. He was carrying a chart and looking around at all of the people when he spoke: "Is there a Mrs. Grant Johnson in the room?"

"Doctor, I'm Mrs. Johnson," I said as I grabbed Clark's hand. Coach Dickerson followed behind me, as Shannell remained sleeping in my arms oblivious of the night's events.

"Mrs. Johnson, my name is Doctor Mitchell. Your husband is going to need surgery on his right knee. His ligaments and a few tendons have been torn away from his kneecap. When your husband arrived at the hospital he was in severe pain. We have given him some pain medication to relax him and he is sleeping at the moment."

"Is he going to be all right?"

"Physically yes, but mentally I don't know."

"Doctor, what are you talking about? There has never been anything wrong with my husband's state of mind."

"Mrs. Johnson, I'm afraid Grant will never play basketball again. With such a severe injury to his knee he is going to need months of physical therapy. The chances of him re-injuring his knee, if he plays again are great and it will cause him to have permanent damage."

"Can I see my husband?"

"Yes, of course. I'll take you to his room if you follow me."

"Coach, you can go home. We will be alright."

"Nonsense, Unique, I'm staying with you until Grant gets out of surgery. I hope you don't mind but I took the liberty of calling my wife, Bethany. She is on her way here to take the kids back home with her if that is okay with you. We are in for along night."

"I…I… don't know. My children might cry. Your wife is a stranger to them. I don't want to impose."

"Don't worry, Unique. My wife is very capable. We have eleven children."

"Oh…okay. Well, I guess they will be all right. Yes, that will be fine. I won't have to worry about them. Thank you."

"You're very welcome, Unique. Here, give me that sleeping angel and Mr. Clark. We'll just mosey on over to the lounge and watch some television until my wife gets here. I'll come and find you when Bethany arrives so you can meet her and kiss the kids goodbye."

"I think it will be best if I say my goodbyes now. Clark honey, look at Mommy. You and your sister are going to go home with the Coach's wife, Miss Bethany. Mommy will come and get you in the morning. Okay?"

Slowly, Clark shook his head in agreement. I kissed him and Shannell goodbye and shook Coach Dickerson's hand. I then turned my attention to Doctor Mitchell who was patiently waiting for me.

"I'm ready, doctor."

"Very well, please follow me."

Dr. Mitchell and I slowly walked down the hall of the disinfected hospital. I hated hospitals. They were too sterile and drab for me.

"Mrs. Johnson, here we are. I'll be back in a moment so you can sign the papers for his surgery."

"Okay, thank you doctor."

"I'll give you some privacy."

I walked to Grant's bed. He looked so peaceful. I gently kissed his lips. Although his leg was wrapped I could see how swollen it was. My heart broke as I realized Grant's lifelong dream of becoming a professional basketball player had been crushed. "My God, how am I going to tell him?"

"Um…tell me what?"

"Grant, you're awake? You scared me. How do you feel?"

"Right now, I feel great. They gave me some kick butt drugs."

"That explains why you are grinning."

"Probably, so what do you have to tell me?"

"Grant you should get some rest." I tried to avert Grant's eyes.

"Unique, I know when there is something wrong with you. Spill it."

"Grant, I…I…"

"I know it's my knee, right?"

"Yes, it…is…"

"I know Unique; you don't have to tell me. When I heard my knee crunching in my ears, I knew I was hurt pretty bad."

"Grant, you must have surgery to repair your knee and…"

"Unique, you are scarring me! What else is it? Are the kids all right? Have you heard from my mother? Is something wrong with her or the kids?"

"Grant, calm down, I think those drugs are getting the best of you."

"Then tell me what is wrong. I can see the fright in your eyes."

Before I could answer, Dr. Mitchell walked in. I was somewhat relieved.

"Grant this is Doctor Mitchell. He will be operating on you."

"Doctor, maybe you can tell me exactly what is wrong with my knee. I know my wife is not telling me the entire truth."

"Grant, honestly I was trying to but I couldn't find the right words." I began to cry.

"Doctor, tell me, now!"

"Mr. Johnson, please, calm down."

I walked over to the other side of Grant's bed and held his hand. Doctor Mitchell fidgeted before he spoke.

"Mr. Johnson, you have ruptured the anterior cruciate ligament or what we refer to as the ACL."

"I don't understand."

"Mr. Johnson, this ligament is one of the most important ligaments in the knee. Its main function is to provide stability to your knee thus minimizing the stress across the knee joint. When you landed on the floor, you twisted your entire kneecap around to the back of your leg. The ACL is completely torn. Did you hear a popping or some refer to it as a crunching sound?"

"Yes, doctor, I did."

"Well, that's common in cases like this. We need to completely replace the ACL. You also tore some other minor ligaments and tendons. We can repair the torn ligaments and tendons then we can reattach them to your kneecap. You will have to endure months of intensive physical therapy…"

"Doctor, what does this ACL actually do?"

"Well, Mrs. Johnson, the ACL provides about ninety percent of the stability to the knee joint. If your husband doesn't get his knee repaired, he will continue to be in excruciating pain and his leg will always feel like it is giving out."

"Doctor, I don't want to hear this entire mumble jumble. Just fix the knee so I can get back to playing ball. I'll do whatever it takes to get back on the court. I figure I will be out of commission for a while. So doc, what time frame are we talking about? My guess is about three months off, max."

"Mr. Johnson I'm sorry but…"

"But what doctor? What are you trying to say? Be straight with me. Can I play ball again?"

"I'm sorry, Mr. Johnson, that is not an option."

"Noooooooo! Damn it no!"

I lay against Grant's chest as he held me tight. We both cried until the nurses took Grant to the operating room.

"Bye honey. I'll be right here when you wake up. I love you."

"I love you too, Unique. We are going to be all right. I guess my law degree is going to come in handy."

"Shush, don't you worry about a thing. Grant, concentrate on getting well. We will take it one day at a time."

"Love you, wife."

I blew a kiss at Grant as the nurses rolled his gurney onto the elevator. I said a prayer as I watched the elevator doors close behind my husband. "God, you are the doctor of all doctors, the healer of all. Please be in the operating room with Grant and guide the surgeon's hands. Repair and heal my Grant. Give him strength in the name of Jesus. Amen."

Chapter 16

After months and months of physical therapy, Grant and I experienced an unexpected surprise. I found out I was pregnant with our third child. Clark was now five, starting kindergarten, and Shannell was experiencing her terrible two's.

On March 14, 1983 exactly at midnight, Isaiah Elijah Johnson was born. He weighed ten pounds and five ounces. He was a handsome baby boy. Unlike his siblings, Isaiah was born with only five strands of hair on top of his head. He looked like a chocolate Milk Dud. Isaiah weighed a little more than my body could handle so I ended up having a cesarean.

Isaiah was definitely an unexpected blessing. I had been taking birth control pills but switched from a high dose to a low dose pill thus resulting in our newest edition to the family.

Grant was now in his first year of law school. When he wasn't in class, he was clerking for Judge Houston.

Since Judge Houston married us, he had been keeping a close watch on Grant's basketball career. When the word got out that Grant would never be a professional basketball player, Judge Houston called Grant and offered him a job at his law office. Grant would be paid as a clerk and mentored by the Judge. In return, Grant promised Judge Houston that when he finished law school and passed the bar exam he would stay on and practice at the Judge's firm.

Christmas 1985 was not only the birth of Jesus but it was also the birth of our last child. Lorna Danielle Johnson was born via another "C" section. She weighed five pounds and two ounces. Lorna was a beautiful baby girl. Her skin tones were reddish brown and she had a head full of wavy black hair.

Lorna was welcomed into our family by her big brothers and her sister. The kids couldn't get enough of her. Shannell was always trying to carry her around. She called Lorna her baby.

All in all, our family seemed to be headed toward a life full of good times. We were blessed with four beautiful children who were healthy and strong.

We were gainfully employed and our careers were moving right along. I must admit it was very difficult to raise a family while working. It seemed like there was not enough hours in the day to get everything done.

We still had not heard from Mrs. Johnson. Grant had finally accepted the fact she and the triplets would never be in his life again. It was a sad state of affairs. I prayed that one-day Mrs. Johnson would come to her senses. She was missing out on the wonderful experience of watching her grandchildren grow and develop. They were growing like weeds every day. One of the kids was getting taller, another one was losing a tooth, or one was experiencing a new adventure.

Time just kept rolling on and on. I felt like I had missed a lifetime with Ruby and Char. Over the past few years we could never get our families together.

I only spoke to Ruby and Char on special occasions like Christmas and birthdays. It has been years since the three of us were in the same room. When I called my girls Ruby always connected us with Char via a three way. I guess some things never changed.

Ruby was doing extremely well and was still living in Atlanta Georgia as she completed the last year of her residency program. She had a two-year-old little boy named Rufus. He was appropriately named after Ruby's favorite group, Chaka Khan and Rufus. I was sure as Rufus got older he was going to hate that name. Ruby had always been special.

Char, as expected was living the life of luxury. Char lived in Detroit and was a marketing vice president at the Kodak Corporation. She was married to Douglas Banks, a scientist who was her college sweetheart. Yes, Douglas was the man who she met many years ago at the Morehouse frat party. Just think if I was on the phone with her just five minutes longer some other woman might be married to him now. Funny, how life worked out.

Douglas and Char had three sons and one daughter. There was Prince, Morris, Luther, and Donna. What's up with my girls naming their children after entertainers?

The last time I spoke to my best friends was right after Lorna's birth. We decided all of us needed some well deserved down time. So we planned a trip to the Bahamas. We were going to go by ourselves. No husbands and definitely no kids. For five days, our life was going to be just like old times it would be just the three of us, three amigos until the end of time.

By the time I got off of the phone with my sisters, my heart was overflowing with excitement and anticipation but again life had something else in store for me…

Chapter 17

February 22, 1986 was not just another typical day in the Johnson household. Indeed, it was a very special day. It was the day our family celebrated the eighth birthday of our eldest child, Clark.

At the crack of dawn, Clark was downstairs in the family room opening up his beautifully wrapped birthday presents. I could hear him scream with joy when he spotted his shiny new red bicycle. Clark had been asking for a new bike for months.

When we finally dragged ourselves out of bed, Grant and I found Clark riding his new bike in the house. Yes, he rode the bike in the house around the dining room table over and over again. I wasn't too upset since it was way too cold for anyone to be outside for any length of time. What a big mistake! I thought I would have to flatten Clark's tires just so I could get the house ready for his party.

Clark absolutely adored balloons so I decorated each room of the house with big, beautiful, colorful balloons. Clark was so keyed up about his party he could barely contain himself, thus causing a chain reaction in Shannell and Isaiah. My children acted like they took an overdose of speed. They just had too much adrenaline. Even little Lorna was unusually fussier than normal.

I was expecting six of Clark's classmates between noon and one, so they could partake in the day's festivities. I made hot dogs; bake beans, and French fries for lunch. For dessert I had two of Clark's favorite things, chocolate ice cream and marble cake with chocolate butter cream frosting I ordered from the grocery store's bakery.

As an extra surprise, I hired a clown who performed various magic tricks. Clark and his friends were in awe of the magical acts. They were absolutely thrilled. The clown finished up his show by making animals out of balloons. The kids exploded with joy.

Isaiah, on the other hand, was afraid of the clown. He screamed and hollered every time the clown attempted to come near him. Shannell loved him and Lorna just sat in my lap and giggled the entire time.

Grant was no help because he was already at work. He had to prepare some legal briefs for a case Judge Houston was hearing. So I was solo at least until three.

The party turned out to be one of the best ones I have ever planned. All of the kids had such a good time. A few of them wanted to spend the night but I just wasn't up to it. By the time Clark's party was over, I was wiped out.

I was completely exhausted from running after ten kids for nearly four and a half hours. I started to feel very ill. I thought maybe I felt sick from being overly tired but I started to get extremely cold and my face felt flushed.

Grant, as expected, didn't make it home by three. I think it was more like six-thirty. I was busy cleaning up the family room when he arrived. I could hear the kids screaming for him as he walked thru the front door.

"Hey birthday boy, come and give your Daddy a big hug. I'm sorry I missed your party."

"That's okay, Daddy. At least you got up this morning to watch me open up some of my presents."

"Well, I have one more present for you."

"Yeah…another present? Where is it Daddy? Where?"

"It's in the closet."

"Oh… boy. I've got another present I can't believe it."

Clark frantically raced to the closet and opened the door. He found the gift and snatched the wrapping paper off.

"Daddy, you got me a bowling ball. It's just my size. Now I can go bowling with you and Mommy. When are we going? Can we go tonight?"

"Son, I'm sorry but your old man is so tired. I had such a long day. Let's go tomorrow afternoon. Does that sound good to you?"

"Okay…Daddy, I guess. Well, you better get some rest because I'm going to beat you and Mommy!"

Grant and Clark laughed together. "Keep dreaming, son."

Grant reached down to pick up Clark as he proceeded to smother him with kisses. Clark squirmed trying to wiggle out of his father's strong arms. Grant gave him a tight hug before releasing him.

"I love you, son."

"I love you, too."

"Where is your Mother?"

"She's in the family room, cleaning up the mess."

Grant patted Clark on the head and walked toward the family room.

"Unique."

"Hey baby. How was your day?"

"It was work. I'm sure I would have had more fun with you and the kids. I'm sorry I had to leave you and it took longer than I expected. I swear Judge Houston has me working like an indentured slave. Sometimes, I feel like I made a deal with the devil. I think he sleeps in his office. I can't work that many hours I need to see my family."

"Aw… baby we aren't going anywhere. You do what you have to do. You know Judge Houston is just set in his ways and he's not the devil Grant. You are simply just overworked. I truly understand your job situation. I know it must be tough being the new kid on the block. I know when you learn the ropes and get your degree one day you'll be bossing a clerk around. I really didn't count on you being here today. I know Judge Houston has you working like crazy but you are learning so much. You are going to be a brilliant attorney."

Grant hugged me from behind and kissed my neck. "I sure hope so. I need to start making some big money."

"All in due time my husband, all in due time. Don't be so impatient. Good things come to those who wait. When God is ready for you to handle your blessing and walk into your season you will have everything you have ever wanted."

Grant was still snuggled up against my backside. "Unique, I thought you knew."

"Knew what?" I said as I slightly turned my head to face his direction.

"I thought you knew I have everything I ever wanted right here with you. You and the kids are my life. I can't imagine my life without you."

I completely turned around to face Grant. We were now face to face and I threw my arms around his neck. "Oh, Grant, I couldn't live without you."

We kissed passionately before we broke our embrace. Grant looked intently in my eyes before he spoke. "You won't have to, Unique, my wonderful, beautiful, and sexy wife, because I plan on tapping that booty for many years to come."

"Grant boy, you are so crazy."

"Guilty as charged. I'm hopelessly and crazy in love with you, Unique Blackman Johnson. I love you."

"I love you too."

Grant and I embraced again as he tenderly pecked my lips. For a second time that evening he slipped his warm tongue in my mouth but this time he immediately pulled back.

"Unique, are you sick? I know you're a hot momma but girl those lips are suddenly on fire."

"Well, I feel a little out of sorts. I think I'm coming down with a cold or something. I really do feel drained and out of whack. I started feeling weird toward the end of the party."

Grant released himself from my arms and stepped back. He looked at me attentively.

"Woman, your face is flushed and pale. I say you're a bit peeked. Unique, you are not cleaning another thing. You go and get in the bed."

I walked toward the couch for fear I was about to faint. "Grant I can't. I need to clean up this mess. Plus, I have to give Lorna and Isaiah their baths."

I was almost at the couch when Grant stepped in between me and the couch. He pointed toward the upstairs. "Unique, I am very capable of cleaning up the house. I can finish in here and get the kids ready for bed. Go on now. I think there is some Tylenol in the upstairs medicine cabinet."

I tried to plead my case. "But Grant, you just got home. I know you are worn out. Honestly, I can finish."

I pouted and picked up a paper plate off of the coffee table. Grant gave me a stern look. The look he gives the kids when he is about to scold them. "Unique…"

"Are you sure?"

"I insist."

"Okay, since you insist I'm going. Are you absolutely positively sure you don't need my help?"

"Goodnight, Unique."

"Goodnight, Husband. I love you. Have fun. Night, kids."

They all replied in unison, "Night, Momma."

And then there was Isaiah sitting on the bottom of the steps. "Momma, Momma, give me a kiss."

"Aw…Isaiah honey, Mommy is sick. How about I just blow you a kiss? I don't want you to catch my cold."

With the biggest bright eyes Isaiah pleaded. "No, Mommy! I want a big juicy kiss."

"Honey…"

"Isaiah!"

"Yes, Daddy?"

"Boy, go sit down somewhere and leave your Mother alone. She can give you a big juicy kiss when she is feeling better."

"Okay, Daddy. Goodnight, Mommy. I love you."

"I love you too, son."

I slowly climbed the ten stairs to our bedroom. My legs were wobbly and felt like I climbed twenty steps. A good night's rest was probably all I needed. I went to our medicine cabinet in hopes of some medication that would make me feel better only to find a drop of children's cherry cough syrup.

I dragged myself back down the hall and leaned over the banister so I could talk to Grant.

"Grant, honey."

"What is it, Unique?"

"There is no Tylenol up here. Do you mind going to the drug store for me?"

"No problem. I'll go. Let me get the kid's coats. I'll take them with me."

"Grant it's not necessary for you to take the kids. It's almost eight and Lorna and Isaiah should be in the bed. Besides, it's too cold out there. Leave the kids home."

"Unique, you ran yourself ragged putting together a wonderful party for Clark. Now you need your rest. I can handle my kids."

"But Grant…"

Busybody Isaiah chimed in. "I want to go, Daddy."

"Isaiah, all of us are going. Clark help you sister's with their coats."

Clark immediately obeyed his father's instructions. "Okay, Daddy. Daddy, can we have some ice cream?"

"Boy, didn't you just have some ice cream about two hours ago?"

Solemnly and with his head hung low Clark responded. "Yes sir, I actually had two scoops."

Grant chuckled. "Boy, go and get your coat on. Look Unique, I'll make a bet with you, if your temperature is normal then the kids stay home with you. If it's over a hundred then you get in the bed and don't move for the rest of the night. The kids and I will be right back. Deal?"

"Deal…"

"Good."

I sluggishly walked back toward the bathroom to retrieve the thermometer. As I waited for the three minutes to pass for my temperature to register, I could hear Grant and the kids scrambling about as they put on their coats and boots. The thermometer beeped and I went back to the banister to tell Grant he had won our bet.

"Okay, Grant, you win. I have a temperature of one hundred two, point five."

"Unique, instead of going to the drugstore maybe I should take you to the hospital."

"Grant I'll be fine. You know I hate hospitals."

"I'm telling you now Unique, if the Tylenol doesn't help you to feel better and doesn't break your fever, then you are going to the hospital in the morning."

"Okay! Hurry back. I'm going to get under the covers right now."

"Good. We should be back in about twenty minutes. Kids say goodbye to Mommy."

The kids gathered at the bottom of the steps and shouted in one accord, "Bye, Mommy we love you."

Shannell walked onto the first step. "Feel better Mommy."

"Thank you sweetie, Shannell Mommy will feel better as soon as I get some medicine."

She rubbed her eyes as she was fighting her bedtime. "You promise, Mommy?"

"Yes, baby I promise."

Shannell chuckled, jumped off the steps and ran toward her siblings who were anxiously waiting at the front door.

Grant opened the front door to usher the kids into the brisk winter night. Before closing the door we exchanged a few pleasantries.

"See you, honey."

"Be careful, Grant. The temperature dropped and the roads are slick."

"Woman, we will be fine. You better be under those covers when I get back and don't you even think about coming back down here to clean up."

"Grant, you know me to well. I was just plotting my course of action."

"Yeah, I know you alright. Love you."

"Love you too."

I peered out the bedroom window as I watched Grant trying to put a fidgeting and feisty Lorna in her car seat while Isaiah and Shannell indulged themselves in a snowball fight. My little man Clark took the opportunity to jump in the front seat of the car so he could sit next to his dad. Grant and Clark were so much alike you would think they were twins. It was really uncanny.

When they pulled out of the driveway, I quickly ran to the bathroom to retrieve my flannel nightgown and tattered rob from the back of the bathroom door. I quickly changed and hurriedly jumped underneath the covers. Ahh…that felt so good. I actually hadn't realized how exhausted I really felt. My body ached from the top of my head to the tip of my big toe. I swear I was asleep even before my head hit the pillows.

****

"Clark."

"Yes, Daddy."

"Did you like your party?"

"Yes, Daddy, I had a great time. Daddy, you missed the clown he was really funny and he did great magic tricks! All of my friends liked him too. I had the best birthday ever! None of my friends ever had a party that was so much fun."

"Well son, you need to thank your Mother for that."

"I will, Daddy, as soon as we get home. I'm going to give her a big hug and tell her she's the best Mommy ever."

"I think she'll like that son. Your Mom is a good woman. Now, what was the clown's name?"

"Oh, yeah the clown. Um…I think his name was JoJo. Look Daddy it's starting to snow again."

"I see it. Look how fast it is coming down. I hope we get back home before it sticks."

"Daddy, those big flakes look like cotton candy. Don't they Daddy?"

"Yes, Shannell. I suppose they do."

"Daddy, when we get home can you help me make a snowman?"

"Clark, you know how to make a snowman. Besides, it's too late to build a snowman and I need to take care of Mommy. But I promise you first thing tomorrow morning we will get up and get outside. Will that work for you?"

"Okay, Daddy, tomorrow it is. Are we still going bowling?"

"Clark if Mommy is feeling better we will go bowling tomorrow afternoon. I see you plan on wearing me out this weekend."

"Yipeeeeeeeeee!"

"Clark, how many times do I have to tell you to put your seatbelt on? You know better."

"Sorry, Daddy. I know you have told me what could happen if we didn't buckle up. We could get really hurt."

"It's okay, son. But let this be the last time I remind you or you will have to sit in the backseat. Is that understood?"

"Yes, sir. I understand."

"Good. I love you and I wouldn't want anything to happen to you or your brother and sisters."

"Da…dee…"

"Yes, Shannell."

"Daddy, Isaiah, he keeps pulling my hair."

"Isaiah you need to stop pulling your sister's hair."

"Daddy, Lorna stinks. She po…pooped."

"Okay, Isaiah. We are almost at the store. I'll change your sister in a minute."

"Yuck, she stinks. Daddy, Isaiah's pulling my hair again." Shannell screamed from the backseat.

"Boy, I told you to stop it! I'm not going to tell you again. If you bother your sister one more time I'm going to spank you! Do you understand me?"

Clark shrieked, "Daddy, watch out…!"

Chapter 18

I was in a deep coma like sleep. It was the type of sleep when you slobber on your pillow; it becomes soaked and you have to turn it over. Without warning and for no apparent reason, I was stirred by some type of jolt. Momentarily, in a daze, I sat up in the bed. I readjusted the covers and lay back down.

About thirty minutes later, my sleep was disrupted again, this time by a loud noise which was coming from downstairs. Boom! Boom! Boom!

"Grant, I think someone is banging on the front door."

I rolled over and there was no Grant. The clock on the nightstand had a time of 9:45 p.m.

"Oh… Grant must be downstairs asleep on the couch. How in the world could he be sleeping with that loud knocking?" "Grant, see who is at the door. I'm too weak to get up. I think my fever has gotten higher."

Still there was no answer. Gingerly, I crawled out of the bed, put on my robe, slipped on my slippers, walked out of the bedroom and into the dark of the hallway.

As I passed Clark's room, I noticed his bedroom door was a jarred. I knew my little man was fast asleep and dreaming of his birthday party. I peeked into his room to make sure he was covered up.

Boom! Boom! Boom!

Damn, why can't Grant get the door? "Just a moment, I' coming." I shouted just before I looked in on Clark. Hmm…Clark was not in his bed. He must be downstairs watching television with his dad. Grant must have decided to give Clark an extra treat, by allowing him to stay up past his bedtime. I bet the two of them were curled up on the sofa with a blanket and the television was probably watching them.

I walked past the other bedrooms and my children were not there.

Boom! Boom! Boom!

I was descending down the steps, when I got a really unexplainable weird feeling. My knees began to knock against each other and my stomach started to flip flop. I tightly grasped the banister to steady my footing. I cautiously and slowly took each step down the stairs. As I made my descent to the first floor of the house, my intuition started to go into overdrive.

My home suddenly felt like it had taken on a life of its own. The house felt mysterious and very eerie. Out of nowhere, a chill swept up the steps. The house was pitch black and awfully quiet. As I continued to go down the steps, I noticed I don't hear the television.

Boom! Boom! Boom! That time I jumped at the sound coming from the door. Where is my family? They should have been back by now.

Boom! Boom! Boom! I apprehensively walked toward the door.

"Who is it?" I said as I turned on the living room lamp.

A strong and powerful voice answered from the other side of the door. "It's the Pittsburgh police."

"What, the police?"

"Yes, Miss, it's the police," a woman replied.

"I am going to keep the latch on the door but I will unlock the door just enough so you can show me some identification."

"That won't be a problem," the husky voice replied.

Hmm…why are there two cops out there? "What in the world could be going on?" I proceeded to open the door slightly, just enough to see the officer's badges.

Satisfied their identification was legit I closed the door, took off the latch and invited my unwelcomed guests in. There stood two of Pittsburgh's finest.

The police woman was so petite I couldn't imagine her arresting anyone. Her partner, however, was a strong and heavily built looking man who was at least six feet tall.

Before I spoke to the officers, I swallowed hard enough to push back the huge lump that had invaded my throat. "Officers may…may… I help you?"

The petite police officer placed her hand on her belt which held her gun. "Are you, Mrs. Grant Johnson?"

"Yes, I am." I said as I adjusted my robe. "What is this about?"

The husky police officer looked at me and my legs wobbled. "Mrs. Johnson, do you own a navy blue 1976 Honda Accord, license plate number GUJ1515?"

"That…that…is my husband's car. Why? What happened? Where are my husband and my kids?"

The petite officer's eyes were sorrowful. She spoke compassionately. "Mrs. Johnson, I'm afraid I have some bad news."

"Bad news!" I screeched at the top of my lungs. I could feel my face getting hotter. My stomach was getting very nauseous.

The husky officer approached me. "Mrs. Johnson, there's been an accident."

"What kind of accident? Where is my family?"

The husky officer grabbed my arm. "That's why we are here. Mrs. Johnson, you need to come with us."

"Go with you? Where? Where is my family?" I began to cry hysterically. Automatically without any thought my body trembled with fear.

The petite officer swallowed a lump that was now in her throat. "Mrs. Johnson, perhaps you would like to sit down on the sofa."

I frantically shook my head in a back and forth motion. "I'm fine right where I am. Please, you are frightening me. I beg you to tell me what happened to my family."

The husky policeman cleared his throat and spoke. "Mrs. Johnson, your husband and children were in a car accident."

"No! Dear God noooo…!" I screamed and screamed again.

The petite officer walked toward me and I collapsed in her arms. "Mrs. Johnson, would you like me to get you a glass of water?" I slowly shook my head no.

The husky officer pulled out a handkerchief and handed it to me.

"Is my family okay?"

The petite officer tried to usher me toward the stairs. "Mrs. Johnson, you need to get dressed so we can take you to the hospital."

"You still haven't answered me. Is my family okay?"

The petite officer's eyes were filled with distress. "Mrs. Johnson, we were dispatched here to this residence to get you. All we know, there was an accident at the intersection of Frankstown and Verona Road. Your family has been rushed to Shadyside Hospital. Please Mrs. Johnson we need you to hurry up and gather your belongings."

"The accident happened at the intersection of Frankstown and Verona Road? My God, that is less than ten minutes away. My husband and the kids…they…they were just going to get me some medication. No! This must be a mistake. Officer, you must be mistaken. They were only going to the drugstore. No! Nothing could happen to them so close to home. Maybe you're at the wrong house. Maybe you misidentified the make of the car. Maybe it was a black Honda and you have the license plate numbers mixed up. Yes, that's what has happened. You'll see. My husband and kids will be walking through the front door at any moment. Just wait...just wait and see."

The petite officer was still holding me up. She turned me toward her and looked intently into my eyes. "Mrs. Johnson, I'm sorry there is no mistake. Please go and get dressed. I can assist you if you want."

"No, thank you, that won't be necessary. I'll be right back."

I ran upstairs and quickly dressed. Tears were escaping my eyes by the gallons. I feared something was terribly, terribly wrong. While I frenziedly dressed I felt my soul cry out with an unimaginable sob which bellowed in the pit of my stomach. I knew in my heart my family was in grave danger and nothing or no one would ever be the same again.

Chapter 18

The police officers drove to the hospital with great speed. Sirens blasted the airwaves and red lights rapidly flashed as we passed by hundreds of cars. We flew down many streets running every stop sign and light.

I bounced around in the backseat of the old dilapidated police cruiser as I silently prayed to God. "Dear God, I know you have the power to heal and mend. Please dear Lord please I beg you to work on my family. Don't let them…Amen."

Within minutes, we arrived at the emergency entrance of Shadyside Hospital. The hospital was crowded with all sorts of people who were sick and suffering. My legs wobbled like Jell-O as the police officers dragged me over to the reception area.

The petite police officer spoke to one of her comrades and they ushered me into an examination room. No one was saying a word but I could look in their faces and know bad news was headed my way.

The petite officer looked at me and said, "Mrs. Johnson, in a moment a doctor will be in to see you. We have to leave now. Is there anything I can get you? Is there anyone I can call for you?"

I responded curtly. "No, there isn't anyone. Thank you. Officer, why can't you tell me what happened to my family?"

Before she could respond a doctor walked in followed by a Chaplain as the Officer quietly slipped away onto her next case. At the sight of the Chaplain I fainted. When I woke up, I found myself in a hospital bed and the Chaplin was praying by my bedside. His gentle smile brought little comfort.

"My child, you have awakened."

"Father, where is my family?"

"I'll go and get the doctor for you. Rest my child."

Within a moment, the Chaplain was back with a doctor who didn't look old enough to practice medicine. He approached my bed with a glum face.

"Mrs. Johnson, my name is Doctor Foster. I am the attending doctor in the emergency room and I have been overseeing your family's care."

"Doctor, how are they?"

"Mrs. Johnson, I have some bad news."

"No! No! No!" I shouted. Tears effortlessly streamed again as I adjusted myself to a full sitting position in the bed.

"What happened? I want to be taken to my family right now!"

"Mrs. Johnson, please I need you to calm down or I will have to give you a sedative."

I was deranged. Anger and fear had taken control of my mind. "You calm down! I want to see my family. Father, please take me to them."

"My child, you need to listen to the doctor. Then I will escort you to see your children."

My mind could not grasp what the Chaplain just said. Did I hear him correctly? Did he just say I could see my children? What? What about my husband? Oh…my God no…!

"Doctor, where is my husband? I need to see him right away! Then we can get our children and get out of here!"

Dr. Foster shifted from one foot to the other. "Mrs. Johnson, how much do you know about the accident?"

"I just know my family was involved a car accident. The officers who picked me up didn't give me much information. My God, Doctor, why won't you tell me what has happened to my family?"

"Mrs. Johnson, this is what I have been told by the first responders, the police officers who were called to the scene of the accident. Apparently, a drunk driver ran a red light and hit your family's car head on as they were crossing the intersection."

"My God, no! Please God, no…!"

The Chaplain moved in closer so he could hold my hand.

"Mrs. Johnson, the impact was great. Your husband's seatbelt wasn't strong enough to hold him. Your husband went through the windshield of his car and landed on the hood of the other car. He then rolled off and fell to the ground. When he landed, he fell on his neck thus breaking it and his spinal column killing him instantly. I'm sorry he was pronounced dead at the scene."

I hysterically wailed at the top of my lungs. "No! No! No! No! Doctor why you are lying to me? No, this can't be true. My husband just went to the drugstore to pick up some medication for me. I wasn't feeling well. Grant and the kids should be home by now. I've got to get out of here. They are probably waiting for me."

I was in complete denial. I tried to get out of the bed but Doctor Foster placed his strong hand on my shoulder and pushed me back down.

"Mrs. Johnson, you can't go home. Your children have sustained serious injuries which I need to explain to you. The gravity of your children's condition must be addressed."

"God…no! Doctor, please don't tell me my babies are dead too. Oh, God please don't…"

"Mrs. Johnson, listen to me. They are not dead but they do need your prayers. We will do everything in our power to make them well. Do you understand me?"

"Yes, doctor, I understand please continue. Is there a bathroom? I think I'm going to be ill."

Doctor Foster pointed to the right of the bed. I jumped off of the gurney and rushed to the bathroom. My insides spilled onto the floor and halfway into the toilet. I had the dry heaves for the next five minutes.

Doctor Foster knocked on the bathroom door. "Mrs. Johnson, are you okay? I can prescribe some medication to prevent you from vomiting."

"I'll be right out." I splashed cold water on my face, exited the bathroom and walked toward the waiting doctor and Chaplain.

"Mrs. Johnson would you like a nerve pill. I can prescribe a low dose of Valium for you."

I put my right hand up in protest. "No, not now, maybe later. Please doctor, I'm ready to hear about my children's injuries."

Before speaking to me Dr. Foster cleared his throat, rubbed his balding head, and put on his glasses as he reviewed the paperwork which he held in his left hand. It felt like an eternity before his lips parted to deliver to me the prognosis of my children. "There was a boy in the front seat of your car. He appears to be around eight or nine."

"He's eight today. That's my boy, Clark. Yes, he turned eight today. What happened to him?"

"I am so sorry Mrs. Johnson. He is in critical condition. In order to save his life we had to rush him to the operating room."

I felt as if I was having an out of body experience. This couldn't be happening to me and my family. "He's in the operating room? Dear God, please don't let my boy die. Doctor what is wrong with him?"

"Mrs. Johnson, a piece of the windshield broke off and cut right through Clark's left leg, right above his knee, cutting his femoral artery. If the ambulance had arrived a moment later your son would have bled to death. The ambulance drivers quickly secured a tunicate and administered some medication which slowed down the bleeding. He lost a considerable amount of blood. Your son was unconscious when he arrived. I did obtain an update and I do know the surgeons were successful in stopping the bleeding. However, Mrs. Johnson there is something else…"

Worriedly, I asked. "What doctor? What else is there?"

"Your son is going to need an artificial leg. I am so sorry."

I felt faint again. This was a nightmare. Someone was playing a cruel, cruel, joke on me. God, please wake me!

I had to sit down. This was just too much. "Doctor, you have to save his leg. Clark plays football. This was his first year playing. He was so excited. No! You can't amputate his leg."

"Mrs. Johnson, I wish there was another option but there is no other choice. His leg was already severely severed. There was no way reattachment could have been successful."

My heart was breaking in a million pieces. How will my son recover from this? My…my…other children, how are they?"

"The child who was in the car seat sustained some cuts and bruises from the broken rear window. However, there was a piece of glass which was stuck in her forehead right above her left eye. She is a very fortunate little girl. A few inches lower and she would have lost her sight. She has about fourteen stitches. We need to keep her overnight for observation."

"Shannell…Isaiah…my other babies, are they alive?"

"The other girl in the back seat has a concussion. Your other son has a broken arm. We will be keeping them overnight too."

Thoughts of Grant rushed into my head. I jumped out of my seat. "I need to see my husband."

"Mrs. Johnson, I would strongly advise against that. He sustained some brutal injuries to his body especially the facial area. His body is not in good shape."

Somehow I mustered a stern look and I moved in the direction of Dr. Foster. I pointed my finger at him and he backed up closer to the door. "I don't care what he looks like. I want to see him now! Father, tell him, I need to see my husband. Please Father, help me."

"Calm down my child. I will take you to see your husband."

"Father, were…were you with him when…when Grant died?"

The elderly Chaplin walked toward me and ever so gently grabbed my hand and put some distance between me and Dr. Foster.

"My child, your husband was dead when he arrived at the hospital. But I administered his last rites and read the Psalm twenty-three over his body. Your husband is in heaven now and he is at peace. He's not suffering. He will forever be with you. He will always be your children's guardian angel."

I shook my head in disbelief. "Father, I am afraid this accident is my fault. I should have gone to the store but Grant insisted I go straight to bed. What have I done, Father? What have I done?"

Wearily the Chaplin spoke. "My child, this accident was not under your control. It's not your fault."

I didn't mean to but I screamed at the frail man. "Yes, it is! And I'll believe that until my dying day! Oh…God, I need to see my husband. This can't be happening." I started to moan uncontrollably.

Dr. Foster walked over to me and gently placed his hand on my shoulder. "Mrs. Johnson, please follow me. I'll take you to see your husband. Is there anyone I can call to come and be with you?"

My mind was a complete blank. I couldn't even think of Ruby and Char's name. "No. There isn't anybody."

The Chaplain stood next to me and gave me a hug. "I'll stay with you my child."

We began our journey down the sterile winding corridors of the hospital. The smell of disinfectants consumed the air. In silence we took an elevator down to the ground floor. We walked past the cafeteria, the laboratories, and the in-house hospital drugstore. The winding halls seemed endless. Finally, the doctor stopped in front of room 103.

Doctor Foster ran his fingers through his straggly beard. "Mrs. Johnson, this is our temporary morgue. Your husband is in there. Are you certain that you want to see him?"

I somberly nodded my head yes.

The angelic Chaplain grabbed my hand. "Mrs. Johnson, I can go in with you. It's not hospital policy to allow family members to view bodies by themselves."

I slightly smiled at the Chaplain and Doctor Foster. "No, Chaplain, thank you. I understand the policy but I need to be by myself. If I am going to make it through this tragedy then I need just a few moments. Can't you understand? I promise not to be long."

Begrudgingly, the Chaplin and Doctor Foster relented. I turned away from them and placed my hands on the cold sterling silver doors. My hands quivered like I had been afflicted with Parkinson's disease. I stood still for a moment and took a deep breath. I exhaled as I slowly entered the dimly lit facility.

The morgue was extremely cold. Shudders ran up and down my spine. The hair at the back of my neck stood straight up. The only sound that could be heard inside the large antiseptic room was my high heel shoes which click clacked on the freshly waxed white marble floor. I slowly approached a few bodies. I could see the only identification; a bright orange and white tag with black lettering on the left big toe. Click, clack, click clack. I proceeded to the fourth silver tray which was located in the middle of the room. It indeed held Grant's lifeless body. I was still in a state of doubt. Mystification flooded my mind and it told me I was at the wrong table but my eyes located the strung tag around his big toe. Verification was positive as I read the name G. Johnson number 65225.

I paused unable to move. I was fixated on the crisp white sheet which covered my husband's body. As I attempted to pullback the sheet that covered my Grant's face I moved in slow motion. I hesitated. My eyes diverted to Grant's left hand. Unexpectedly, I found myself hypnotized as I viewed Grant's shiny gold wedding band. The band glowed like it did on the day we purchased it so many years ago.

Out of the blue my mind became inundated with childhood memories. I could clearly see Grant as a little boy bouncing his basketball and walking toward me. Oh… how my heart fluttered. Then there was the first kiss that made me tingle all over and the first night Grant made love to me. My God how could this be? My mind struggled as it was weighed down trying to decipher and rationalize my wonderful dear loving remarkable husband was now a cold corpse. I cannot comprehend my Grant, my one and only true love was now nothing but lifeless flesh. Knowing Grant was forever gone from my life made my heart skip beats as it broke and crumpled.

Still drawn by Grant's wedding band I gingerly took his hand. "My… Lord!" I screamed. His body was not cold but lukewarm. Maybe my prayers were answered and Grant was still alive? This was all a terrible tragedy. Sadly, I was only kidding myself. I could see Doctor Foster and the Chaplin standing at the entrance of the morgue peering through the oversized glass windows. They conversed with each other while keeping their eyes adverted on me.

I took hold of Grant's hand and slowly removed the band from his finger. Miraculously, not a drop of blood was on the ring. I gingerly kissed the symbol of our love. I removed the gold chain from around my neck which held my mother's cross and I added my husband's band onto the necklace. The ring would rest between my bosom and next to my heart until the day I was reunited with my love in heaven.

Tears continued to run with ease down my face as I once again tried to remove the sheet from my husband's body so I could see Grant's face. I reached for it again but stopped.

"My husband can't be in there. No, I don't believe it." I continued to stare at the covered body.

My crying turned into uncontrollable piercing shrills. I wrapped my arms around my body and rocked back and forth. I moaned and for the first time in my life I experienced unruly limbs which trembled and I began to shake non-stop. The Chaplain rushed into the room. He tried to placate me.

"My dear child, perhaps you should do this at another time. Let's go and see your children."

I turned into a crazed lunatic. "Leave me alone! Get out of here! I don't need you to console me! Tell me Father, where was God? Where was God when that drunk driver drove into my family? Where was He?" I screamed at the Chaplain with such cruelty he was taken aback.

"My child…"

"Don't call me your child. I'm not your child. God has forsaken my family and me. Leave me alone! Please just go!"

I collapsed on top of Grant's motionless limp body, which caused the sheet to fall from him. I was absolutely stunned and horrified as I looked at the torn face which was once my incredibly gorgeous husband. Grant's dissected face was almost cut down the middle. His perfect angular nose was now on the left side of his face almost by his ear. His lips were twice their normal size. They were cut, bruised, and distorted. One of Grant's beautiful eyes had popped out of its socket. The strong muscular arms that used to hold me tight in the middle of the night were shredded beyond recognition.

My body convulsed as if on autopilot. I had no control as I felt my body gyrating out of control. I couldn't stand to look at my husband a moment longer. I bawled and bellowed as I fell onto the floor.

Swiftly, a nurse and Doctor Foster ran into the morgue as they struggled to lift my convulsing body. Everyone in my mind was animated and moving very leisurely. To my anguished intellect I was dreaming. This couldn't be happening to me. I was overcome with the most unbearable sorrow I had ever felt in my entire life. Abruptly the world went dark.

Chapter 19

The next thing I knew I was waking up in yet another hospital bed. I awakened to find Doctor Foster standing in front of my bed, reading my chart.

He smiled ever so slightly. "Mrs. Johnson, I'm glad you have finally awakened. I was really worried about you."

Still in a bit of a fog I adjusted myself to a sitting position in the squeaky hospital bed. "What happened to me?"

"You became hysterical and we sedated you. You have been sleeping for the past five hours. I also gave you some medication your fever was at one hundred and four degrees"

"How is my son, Clark?""

"He is in the recovery room and doing very well. He will be moved to intensive care shortly. As I had advised you, he lost a considerable amount of blood but your boy is strong. He's a fighter. The next twenty-four hours are very critical but I believe that Clark will survive. His vitals are getting stronger and stronger. If all goes well, we can measure him for a prosthetic in about two or three weeks. Then he will have to endure months and months of physical therapy. That young man has a long road ahead of him."

I wiped a tear from the corner of my eye. "Does he know his leg is gone? Does he know his Daddy has passed away?"

"Mrs. Johnson, it will be a while before Clark's brain realizes or should I say it registers that his limb is missing. He has been heavily sedated since he arrived here at the hospital and has been unconscious. He doesn't know anything about his father. Besides, it would be inappropriate for me to tell him. I believe that information should come from you."

I struggled to get out of the bed. "I want to see my children."

"Mrs. Johnson, your children are resting comfortably and in your present state of mind, I would advise against it. You should get some rest. I'll come and get you when they awaken."

"I want to see my children now! Why can't I see them? Did they die while I was sleeping? Is that why you want me to rest? Tell me the truth Doctor!"

Dr. Foster swiftly moved toward my direction and tried to get me back into bed. "Mrs. Johnson, honestly I would not lie to you. Your children are resting."

I still was not convinced Dr. Foster was telling me the truth. My voice wavered with fear. "Then I want to see them now!" I jumped out of the bed and almost fell flat on my face. Doctor Foster caught me and eased me onto the edge of the bed.

"Mrs. Johnson, the drugs we have given you have not worn off. Please get back in bed. I'll get a wheelchair and I'll take you to see your children. Please stay in the bed until I get back. Can you do that for me?"

"I will, Doctor. Please tell me my children are alive."

"Mrs. Johnson, I promise you they are alive. I'll be right back."

I felt lightheaded so I scooted back further in the bed and waited for Doctor Foster to return.

As promised Doctor Foster returned. He took me to the intensive care unit to the room of my poor baby Clark. He was lying in the bed with a bunch of tubes coming from his body. Doctor Foster gave me a mask to cover my face then wheeled me next to the bed. I grabbed Clark's hand and kissed it gently.

I couldn't control my tears. I had to pull it together so I could be strong for my son. He didn't need a hysterical mother. "Clark, its Momma. I'm right here. You fight, you hear me boy? You've got to fight. I love you very, very much. Remember that okay my little man?"

I wept some more as Doctor Foster took me to the room that Isaiah and Shannell were sharing. My babies looked like sleeping angels. My Lord, how am I going to tell them about their Daddy?

"Doctor, are you sure they are resting comfortably? I don't want them to be in any pain. They have been through enough."

"You have my word, Mrs. Johnson. They are medicated and resting without any pain."

"Good. Keep them like that as long as you can because they…they are going to hurt some more when I have to…I have to tell them about their daddy."

"Mrs. Johnson, I have called our social services department, they will be sending a Mrs. Netta Peters to help you deal with your grief."

"Doctor, no one can help me with my feelings because I don't know what to do with them."

"Maybe not, but Mrs. Peters, can help you tell the children and she can recommend the best family grief counselors in your area. She can aide you with the preparation of funeral arrangements for your husband."

"Make funeral arrangements? Jesus, I…I…hadn't even thought about it. Doctor, where is my Lorna?"

"She's at the end of the hall, the last room on the right."

Dr. Foster quickly wheeled me to Lorna's room. I was pleasantly surprised. I found Lorna awakened in her crib as she played with a Teddy bear. When she saw me, her eyes lit up and she mumbled, "Momma."

My heart soared with happiness. I rushed out of my wheelchair and grabbed my daughter. I held her tight in my arms and wept.

"Momma's here baby. Momma's here." I stayed with Lorna until she fell asleep again.

I wheeled myself back to intensive care and waited on Clark to wake up. I must have fallen asleep. A soft touch jolted me from my sleep.

"Mrs. Johnson?"

I looked up and saw the slightly wrinkled face of a gray haired mid-seventyish, almond colored woman, with a warm and engaging smile. "Yes, I'm Mrs. Johnson. Who are you?"

"I'm Mrs. Netta Peters, from social services. I'm sorry to disturb you. I know you want to be with your son but can you come into the hallway for a moment so we can talk?"

"Mrs. Peters, I'm sorry you came all this way to see me but I don't need to talk to you. I'm fine."

She gingerly grabbed my hand, caressed it, and sighed. "Please, Mrs. Johnson, I promise I won't take up much of your time. I thought you might be hungry. I hope you don't mind, I took the liberty of buying you a Coke and a turkey sandwich."

I looked at the saintly, Mrs. Peters, and managed to give her a half smile. "Yes, I am a little hungry, thank you."

I kissed Clark on the forehead and whispered in his ear. "Momma, will be right back. I love you."

Mrs. Peters handed me my food and pushed me into the hallway toward a quaint waiting area across from Clark's room. She proceeded to sit down on the hard blue chairs. She peered at me over her gold wire rimmed glasses as I began to devour my sandwich.

"Mrs. Johnson."

I nodded, chewed and shifted the turkey sandwich from one side of my mouth to the other side. I tried to speak to this seemly compassionate woman. "Please, Mrs. Peters, call me Unique."

She slightly chuckled, "Only if you call me Netta."

"Okay, Netta it is."

We both smiled at each other.

"Unique, I'm sincerely very sorry to hear of your loss. I am here to help you and your children get back on your feet. Whatever you need me to do just ask. I am a willing vessel and at your disposal to get you through this difficult time."

"Netta, how do you ever get back on your feet after something as tragic as this? I've been with Grant since I was a child. He is…he was my one and only love."

"Unique, I'm not going to sit here and lie to you. It's not going to be easy. Some days you will feel like giving up but you will go on. You need to take small steps. You need to take one second, one minute, one hour, one day, one week, and one month at a time. I promise you, God will be there with you every step of the way."

"Netta, how can you be so positive I will go on?"

"Unique, you will go on because you have four good reasons to."

"I'm sorry Netta, what are you talking about?"

"Your four reasons to go on are your children. They need you and depend on you to get them through this. They have to deal with the loss of their daddy. It's going to be very traumatic for Clark since he is the oldest. Like you, he will always remember this day. Shannell and Isaiah will have pain but it won't be as great. Overtime, they will adjust and forget some of these events since they are a bit younger than Clark. Lorna will not remember a thing. She'll live vicariously through all of your families' memories. Unique, God will make a way for you. He will give you your strength and peace. All you have to do is ask Him."

"God will make a way? I doubt it! God took away my husband while that son of a bitch…that drunk driver barely got a scratch on him. My oldest boy lost his leg and his daddy all on his eighth birthday and my other children are lying in hospital beds hurting. So forgive me, Netta, if I don't see God in this picture. In fact where has He been all of my life while I lost the people I love the most in this word? Where was he while I was being raised by a part-time verbally abusive father? Tell me Netta, where is my God?"

Netta crossed her legs and sighed. "Unique, He has always been with you. You have to trust Him and keep your faith even when you can't trace him. Unique, I know you are hurting. But…"

I had enough of Netta. I raised my voice, "How do you know what I feel? Are you married? Is your husband still alive? Have your children ever been seriously injured?"

Netta pushed her sliding glasses back on her nose. "Unique, my entire life, I have dealt with many families during troubling times. Social work is my life it is my passion and my purpose. You're totally right I can't feel your hurt because my husband and I have been blessed with a fifty-year marriage. I was never blessed with any children of my own but I can sympathize with you. I am not immune to pain and suffering."

I snapped, "You have no children? Then you really don't have a clue!"

"Unique, God didn't have it in His plan for me to have children. When I was younger, I used to be mad at God. I asked Him why He made me sterile. It's not until I got older and started my social work that God's plan was revealed to me. You see the families and many foster children whom I have helped over the years are my purpose. It's what God has called me to do and it is my reason for being. I keep very busy with helping others. I'm so fulfilled with my work for the Lord I don't miss not having any children. There is nothing I lack because He provides all of my needs."

I felt very ashamed for being so cruel to Netta. At that moment, I realized she was the only person in the world who could help me make some sense of this tragedy.

I swallowed the last bite of my sandwich, gulped the last bit of the lukewarm Coke, and wiped my nose with the crumbled tissue I had been holding for the past few hours. "Netta, I…I apologize for lashing out at you. I'm just so weighed down. Just so…my heart is heavy. I am weary."

"Unique, the Lord says in His word, the book of Matthew chapter eleven verse twenty-eight; Come unto me, all ye that labour and are heavy laden, and I will give you rest. Rest in Him, my Unique, rest in Him."

I broke down. I was mentally and physically drained. Netta held me tight and rocked me in her arms. Briefly, she provided me comfort and soothed my tormented heart.

"There, there, Unique. Let it out. I'm here for you for as long as it takes. You might not want to hear this but God is with you too. He has a purpose for your life which will be revealed in time. The

God I serve is merciful. God has not forsaken you. He will not leave you. He will carry your burden onto Himself."

As my heart continued to break into a million pieces I sobbed chaotically in Netta's arms until the wee hours of the morning. The gentle soul called Netta held me as I slept in the warmth of her embrace. She was really heaven sent.

Chapter 20

Late in the afternoon after I had spoken to the children's doctors, I arrived home from the hospital and began the daunting task of making funeral arrangements. My soul was a broken shell. Netta offered to come home with me to aide in the preparations and make some of the phone calls but I needed space. I wanted time by myself to wrap my head around the fact that the love of my life, the father of my children was gone. I spent half of my life loving Grant. Now what was I supposed to do? Who was going to show Clark and Isaiah how to be a man? Who was going to walk Shannell and Lorna down the aisle? "This is so unfair!" I shouted at the top of my lungs. "We were supposed to grow old together. We were going to travel the world and watch our grandchildren grow up. How could you do this to me? Haven't I suffered enough? What am I to do with this shattered life? Jesus, how dare you, why did you allow this to happen to us?"

My self-absorbed psychotic rant ended when I recognized someone was pounding on the front door and erratically ringing the doorbell.

"I'm coming!" I opened the door and fell into the arms of Ruby and Char.

Ruby and Char practically carried me to the sofa. "How did you know?" I mumbled as we sat on the sofa.

"Unique, you know how news travels through the neighborhood." Char said, wiping away the wet hair that dangled in my face.

Ruby wiped away my tears. "You're not going to believe this but my dad saw the crash. He was coming back from Giant Eagle and drove by the accident not realizing it was Grant's car. Then he heard about it on the local news. He called me and then I called Char. We kissed our families goodbye and caught the first thing smoking home."

"I…I… I can't believe it. Are you really here? Am I dreaming? I've been lost, walking around in circles trying to make sense of everything. Seeing the both of you, I can't believe it."

"Where else would we be, Unique? I know we don't see each other as often as we would like but we love you. We are here to help you for as long as you need us." Ruby said as we all held each other in a group hug.

My best friend's embraced and consoled me with their love. Even though many years had passed and our lives had gone in different directions, our sisterhood, our bond was still solid and indestructible. For the first time, since this unspeakable nightmare started, I had a fleeting moment of normalcy.

Chapter 21

The day we buried Grant was the hardest day of my life. I had buried a lot of people in my lifetime but this time was different. It was surreal. The pain implanted itself in the core of my being and ripped it to shreds from the inside out. My mind was befuddled with fond memories, pain, joy, and sorrow. I was still in a state of disbelief. My world had literally been turned upside down and crushed, like someone threw a bottle up in the air, it hit the ground with a thud and broke into a million small pieces. That's how I felt, smashed into a million small unusable pieces. How do I begin to mend and put together the fragmented pieces of my life?

The service was at Mt. Ararat, the church where Grant was baptized as a child. I don't know how I would have made it if it hadn't been for Ruby and Char who held me up. Ruby flanked my right side and Char was on my left as I viewed Grant's body for the last time. He looked at peace as he lay in the bronze casket. A slight smile graced his now recognizable face. The mortician performed an exceptional job at restoring his facial features; there was not a trace of his previous disfigurement.

As I stood and looked at my beloved, I told myself it really wasn't Grant in the coffin. I knew at any moment he would come running from the back doors of the church, tell me it was all a huge mistake, and I would fall into his arms, never letting him go, but it didn't happen. I inhaled deeply and slowly exhaled as I removed a piece of hair from his forehead and stroked his hair. I leaned into the casket, kissed his cold lifeless lips, and collapsed on top of his rigid chest. Ruby and Char dragged me back to the pew.

The funeral services started around one. My stoic, Clark was seated in his wheelchair at the end of the first pew. He refused to shed a tear. Oblivious, to the day's events, Lorna slept in Char's arms. Netta sat in between Clark and his siblings. The sobs of Shannell and Isaiah tore at my already broken and crushed heart.

I didn't think I could handle anything else. I spoke too soon. Perhaps, the greatest shock of the day was the unforeseen arrival of Mrs. Johnson and the triplets. It had been years since she graced my presence but I knew the now aged Mrs. Johnson anywhere. As she walked down the aisle you could still see the once beautiful and regal woman like the first day I saw her decades ago. The triplets had grown into handsome and striking looking teenagers.

Judge Houston escorted Mrs. Johnson to her son's casket. She wept quietly and kissed her son goodbye. I got up to greet her but Judge Houston intervened and stepped in between us. I was beyond shocked and hurt to say the least. I had loved her like she was my mother. We were sharing the same bleeding wound and unspeakable pain, yet she let someone come between us. I was dumbfounded by her peculiar actions.

Mrs. Johnson nodded in my direction, briefly stopped at the pew, opened her purse, and handed me an envelope as she walked past me. No hug, no words were spoken between us but our souls touched and agreed with our shared grief. The triplet's faces were streaked with tears. They didn't acknowledge me as they walked behind Mrs. Johnson and Judge Houston. I wanted to jump up and cling to her. I wanted a warm, caring, loving embrace, and an explanation as to why she stayed away but she departed as quickly as she had entered the sanctuary.

After we laid Grant to rest, the following days still felt like my life wasn't my own. I was disconnected from reality. Trying to work, taking care of the children and making sure Clark made it to physical therapy three times a week was exhausting. I couldn't sleep at night. When I closed my eyes, visions of Grant lying in the morgue plagued my dreams. I was overwhelmed with heartache and guilt. If I had gone to the drugstore myself, my family would still be intact.

I spoke to Netta on a regular basis, at least twice a week, sometimes more. She always imparted some sort of wisdom into my spirit. Sometimes it was received and most of the times it wasn't.

"Uniquie, God doesn't make any mistakes."

"I'm sorry, Netta but I totally disagree. This time He got it wrong."

She sighed. "My dear, in order for God to begin the healing process, you need to let go of the hurt, guilt, this anger, and depression. You can't blame yourself for circumstances which were out of your control. Now it's time to let go of the pity and look to the hills where your help comes from."

"Netta, I don't want any help. I'm fine right where I'm at. Maybe, I want to wallow is this unbearable anguish. I want to be left alone, to ball up in a corner and die."

"My Darling, Unique, I'm going to pray for you because it's the only thing I know what to do in times of great tribulation."

"You do that, Netta. I don't even know if I can pray for myself."

"Sometimes, Unique all you have to utter is one word."

I was getting impatient. "And what word would that be Netta?"

"Unique, you have to know to call on the name above all names. Just call on Jesus. Just Jesus, he'll search your heart with the utterance of His name."

"Good night, Netta."

"You can run, child but you can't hide. Good night."

"Love you, Netta."

"I love you too but remember who loved you the most when He went to the cross to die for the remission of our sins."

"I know, Netta."

I disconnected our conversation. I was so tiered of Netta preaching the gospel. I would love, just one time, to have a normal conversation with her without the mention of Jesus, God or the Holy Ghost. As far as I was concerned all three failed me.

Chapter 22

It took several weeks for me to read Mrs. Johnson's letter. One night I finally found the courage or should I say liquid courage to read it. After I drank several glasses of Riesling I got into bed and removed the letter from my bible. I looked at the red envelope with the stylish writing.

I sipped the wine and proceeded to read the note. Mrs. Johnson said after the deaths of her husband and mother, the sorrow she felt was too much. She could no longer live in a house full of memories of what used to be her enchanted life. She believed Grant and I had our own lives and we would be better off without her. She had to leave because she felt she was losing her mind and indeed had a meltdown. She confessed, over the last several years she had been diagnosed with Bi-Polar II Disorder with Psychosis and was on medication. The letter went on to say losing her first born child was unfathomable and caused her more pain than the combined deaths of her husband and mother. She had no inner strength to stay for the funeral. She ended her letter simply stated, "No mother should bury her child. It's unnatural and out of order. I love you and hope you find peace."

I don't know if I would ever have peace. I wanted to be a part of Mrs. Johnson and the triplet's life. We needed our family. I couldn't reconcile this cruel reality. How could she not want to deal with us and be a part of her grandchildren's life? It was unimaginable and yet it was very real. How could a loving God strip our family apart and leave us to struggle? How could He abandon us? Where was He, when Grant and my family got into the car? What type of God would allow five children to be left fatherless? Why God, why? No answer…

One Friday night around ten, the kids were nestled in their beds; I was dressed in my favorite tattered purple robe with matching pajamas, getting relaxed and prepared to watch Miami Vice, when there was a knock at the door. "Who could this be, interrupting my date with Tubbs?" I knew no one who would visit me at this late hour. I peeped out the living room curtains. To my disbelief there stood Judge Houston. I slightly opened the door.

"Judge Houston, what brings you by?"

"Hi Unique, please accept my sincerest apology for stopping by so late and unannounced but I was in the neighborhood. I thought I would take a moment and check on you, to see if you and the children were okay. Do you mind if I come in?"

I removed the safety chain from the door. "Of course, Judge Houston, forgive me. Come on in."

Judge Houston rather rudely pushed past me, took off his coat and placed it on the back of the couch. I closed the front door and motioned for the Judge to follow me to the family room. Judge Houston broke the silence.

"Unique, may I have a glass of water?"

"Sure, Judge Houston, have a seat. I'll be right back."

"Unique, please, we don't need to be so formal. You can call me, Randall."

"Okay…" I yelled from the kitchen. I lingered in the kitchen longer than necessary. Uneasiness crept into my spirit and my instincts sounded off in the inside of my soul like a five alarm fire. Something wasn't right.

Judge Houston patted his hand on the couch, "Come sit next to me."

I cautiously sat next to him. "So Judge, I mean Randall, what brings you by?"

"I wanted to see you. I thought you might need someone to help relieve your stress. You know someone to talk too. I am a very good listener. I have to be in my line of work that's part of my job description. So here I am offering you my services for free."

He let out an eerie laugh. I slowly moved away from him and repositioned myself on the couch.

"Randall, I truly appreciate you thinking about me but we, we don't need anything. I don't need any consoling. I don't need anyone to listen to or give me any advice. I am taking it one day at a time."

Judge Houston nodded in agreement as he moved closer to me and invaded my private space. "I know how you are feeling Unique. When my Margaret unexpectedly departed this life and went on home to glory, I felt such an incredible gut wrenching loss. I often found myself wondering from room to room hoping and wishing she would appear in one of those rooms. I even prayed she would be in her office sitting in her favorite chair crocheting or knitting something. For a long time I smelled her perfume lingering in the hallways. I know what it's like to miss the touch of your loved one. I know what it feels like...to feel neglected, to feel abandoned. It's natural to be angry at Grant for not having the will to fight and live. It's natural even if you're mad at God."

"You know Randall, it's late and I am getting sleepy. I think you should leave. I sincerely appreciate you stopping by. It's always to a pleasure to see you."

I tried to get up and move but Judge Houston snatched my hand and inappropriately pulled me into a tight embrace. I could smell the vodka he evidently consumed before he decided to come by. He grabbed the base of my neck and smothered me with his large lips. I tried to wiggle from underneath the weight of his torso but he held me tightly. His warm alcoholic tongue forced its way into my mouth. I felt frightened. Then my tongue with a mind of its own entwined with his. I was ashamed. He felt good. Heat rose in my private area, my breast started to swell. How could I feel something for him? How could I betray Grant? I tried to rationalize my behavior but my body yearned for his touch.

I told him, "Wait," As I tried to compose myself.

"What if my kids come down here?"

"Stop, with the excuses, Unique. You know your kids aren't coming down here. I've wanted you ever since I performed your marriage ceremony. You were absolutely breathtaking. I could've made love to you right then and there. After all these years you haven't aged a bit and you still have such an incredible body. I can't count the numerous times I have pleasured myself with the memory of you."

What? Is this scenario really playing out? I was disgusted with myself as I contemplated having sex with my husband's boss, in my husband's house, with my children upstairs? I was conflicted, until Randall dropped his pants. His oversized member unraveled out of his black and white polka dotted underwear. It pulsated in front of me. I gasped. My juices flowed and moistened my inner thighs. I'd never seen another man's anatomy. Oh, what a glorious magnificent sight. I undressed with great urgency as my mound pulsated against the fabric of my pajama bottoms. Without a single word translating between us, my sweet juice beckoned Randall. We proceeded to the floor and I rode him until the sun came up.

Chapter 23

It was almost 6:00 a.m. when Randall finally awakened from his drunken sex filled slumber. He had the nerve to want to go for it again. After some prodding I got him out of the house.

Thankfully, the kids were still asleep. I quietly crept up the stairs and entered the bathroom. I undressed and filled the tub with the hottest water I could stand. I was beyond mortified by my actions. I submerged my disgusting defiled body into the scorching water. I saturated the green washcloth with a thick lather of Camay soap as I wiped off the filthy stale perspiration which dripped from Randall's intoxicated body. Every pore of my body had been drenched with his spew. His scent embedded itself into my skin. I had to cleanse myself from my unrighteousness. I tried to purge myself from the sickening feelings which percolated in my soul. I had opened the floodgates to the pit of hell.

The thought of his ejaculated seed inside of me caused me to heave. I got out of the tub and quickly grabbed the razor from the medicine cabinet. I returned to the tub and began to slice at my wrists. I watched as the once crystal clear water turned crimson. My mind was relieved. I finally had the courage to leave this desolate existence.

Isaiah shouted and jolted me from my slow descent into the afterworld.

"Momma, I got to pee. Open the door, hurry!"

I shrieked, "Isaiah, don't come in. I don't have on any clothes"

I was humiliated I had contemplated taking my own life. How could I leave my children orphaned? I quickly jumped out the tub, drained it, hurriedly searched the medicine cabinet for bandages, swiftly covered my wrists with gauze, and slipped on my robe.

An impatient Isaiah pleaded from the other side of the closed door, "Momma, please, I'm going to have an accident."

I opened the door and yelled at him as he darted past me to get to the toilet. "Boy, I told you about drinking juice before you went to bed!"

With sorrowful eyes he looked at me them squawked, "Momma, there's blood on your robe."

I tried to play if off. "Oh…no, it's just cranberry juice I accidently spilled. Mommy can be so clumsy at times. Now, hurry up, wash your hands and get to bed."

Not quite convinced by my explanation but to sleepy to ask any further questions or continue the conversation, he conceded, "Oh…okay." He walked back down the hall toward his bedroom.

I was relieved to hear his bedroom door shut. I sat on the edge of the tub for hours as I tried to figure out why I wanted to commit suicide. I was beyond lost.

After attempted suicide and my torrid affair with Judge Houston it weighed heavily on my conscience. I felt disgraced. Grant was the only man I had been intimate with until Judge Randall Houston. Was I out of my mind? He was old enough to be my grandfather but yet he had the body of a man half his age. I felt emotions and experienced positions I never encountered with Grant. I enjoyed the new experiences yet I felt I dishonored my husband's memory.

Life as I knew it had completely vanished. The tryst with Judge Houston started a deteriorating new chapter of my life. I accepted my out of control fate because I needed to escape my life's dreadful existence. I believed I deserved a bad life because I would never amount to anything. Everything the enemy told me I accepted. I was sin sick. I walked away from God because He had turned His back on me.

I started to frequent night clubs, bars, and the strip joints on a weekly basis. I looked for unattached and attached men who wanted to go a hotel, have a good ole time with no fear of an emotional bond. I found myself consistently asking Netta to watch the kids as I often dropped them off at her home and brought these strangers to my house because the hotel costs started to put a dent in my finances.

Each time I went out on the prowl I felt like I was in someone else's body. I fantasized about my next victim's physical attributes. I wondered what their member looked like underneath their clothes. My sexual fantasies kept my mind occupied so pain and grief stayed away. I allowed myself to play in Satan's playground of sexual immorality. I loved every minute of it. I no longer knew myself as I sunk further and further into the pit of hell.

Stalking my next conquest made me flush with hot desire. The excitement of it all made my heart race with anticipation. Who would I pick out of the crowd for my next escapade? Who would satisfy my new hunger for sexual healing?

I really wasn't prejudiced. I liked them all. Whether they were tall, short, dark, light, skinny or fat it didn't matter to me. As long as I got sexed up and received some money to pay a few bills, all was right in my world, so I thought. Truthfully, I was spiraling out of control. The only difference between me and a hooker was…well really there was nothing. I tried to convince myself that after the deed was done I wouldn't do it again. Unfortunately, I was addicted to the temporary pleasure I longed for. My new lifestyle meant I had to step up my fashion sense. I purchased the appropriate clothes and some gorgeous stilettos which accentuated my long strong legs. I learned very quickly, men loved long sexy legs in a good pair of high heels. Of course my round behind, tiny waist, and ample breasts made me the perfect combination of any man's fantasy.

It seemed like an eternity as I stalked every nightclub and dive within the vicinity of Pittsburgh and its surrounding areas. My favorite hangout destinations were located in Ohio, Youngstown and Shaker Heights to be exact.

My erotic escapades made me a scholar. I earned a PhD. in the physical characteristics of the male sex organ. I could tell you the length and width of my partner's tool even before he took off his clothes. If he didn't make the cut, I quickly came up with an excuse to break our date. I figured why drop the panties if my fingers could do the walking.

I went through a ten-year period of a self-destructive, unprotected, sex life which I called the alphabet stage. I literally slept with the entire alphabet. There was Adam, Brent, Cameron, Denny, Edward, Frank, Gill, Hillary (don't ask that's another story), Inez, Jacob, Kevin, Lonnie, Mark, Neal, Oscar and Paul. Then there was bisexual Quinton, Rob, Sam, Terrance, Unger, Victor, Walter, Xander, and Yael. Yael was an Israeli who claimed his name meant God's strength. That may be true but trust me when I tell you his bedroom skills had no strength! Not one ounce. Weak was more like it. He lasted all of two hours.

Then there was Zion. Yes, the mighty, mighty strong Zion. I found Zion by accident. He worked at a construction site near the bank. I remembered every moment of that day. It was about one hundred degrees in the shade. In that type of weather with the humidity you were soaking wet before you even walked to the next block. I wasn't paying any attention to where I was going. My mind was on how I was going to get out of the heat and where I was going to eat. I hadn't eaten breakfast and I was starving.

Hurriedly, I walked down Fifth Ave. and accidently ran into this man who had an incredible rock solid chest.

"Excuse me." I stated quickly. I regained my composure and began to walk away. I hesitated and got a good look at Zion. He made my knees weak. Zion's physique was flawless. His body was like Zeus, one of the Greek gods. He was a masterpiece of pure perfection. The muscles of his biceps rippled from beneath his cut off, form fitted light blue top. Three buttons on his shirt were undone, displaying beads of sweat which dripped down his six-pack. He flashed a wide grin of perfectly aligned, sparkling, pearly white teeth. On the left side of his face set a deep dimple.

He asked, "Miss, are you okay? I'm sorry for running into you. It's been a long day. I wasn't paying any attention to the lunch time crowd."

"Umm…yes. Yes, I'm fine. Thank you. Mr…?"

"McPherson. But you can call me Zion."

"Zion McPherson, the pleasure is mine."

"And what is your name?"

"My name is Unique Johnson." I said to him as I bated my eyes and extended my right hand.

His huge hand engulfed mine. Our sweat mixed, hormones activated, and the primal carnal desire which dwelled deep inside our secret place ignited. I started to perspire profusely.

"Is that Miss or Mrs. Johnson?"

"It's Mrs."

"Oh…" Zion said quickly. He disconnected our hands and looked rejected like the Steelers defensive line had just tackled him in the final seconds of the Super bowl.

"Well, Zion, actually I could be considered a Miss."

"What? I'm not following you. Are you going through a divorce or something?"

"No, I am a widow."

"Oh…wow. I'm sorry."

"No need to be sorry, but thank you. Look Zion, I have to get out of this intolerable heat. I don't know how you work out here all day long."

"It's not that bad. I've been in construction since I was eighteen. I'm used to all the elements. Besides, the money makes up for any discomfort."

"I see. Look, I'm going to get my lunch. Maybe, I'll see you around town."

"I would like that, Unique. I'll be on this construction project for another two weeks. Perhaps, we can go to lunch this week? That's if you don't mind being seen with a man who has some dirt on him."

My mind wondered as I looked at the strapping, well-built, burly arms and visualized myself swinging from them. I was transitorily lost with my nasty thoughts.

"Unique."

"Yes, what were you saying?" Oh…yes, lunch. Lunch would be fine. Here is my number." I handed him my business card and sashayed away making sure every curve of my backside swung with precision from side to side.

Chapter 24

After our first lunch date Zion and I became inseparable. We spent all our time together. We went to the movies, ate at some exquisite restaurants and enjoyed the nightlife. Zion really knew how to make a woman feel like a queen and the sex… well let's say it was beyond spectacular. He was packing in all the right places. His elongated tongue performed magic tricks on my pulsating mound. Every woman should have a Zion experience.

Before I knew it Zion was moving into the home I once shared with Grant. The kids adored him. He was an exceptional father figure and he spoiled them with all sorts of gifts. Of course he became their "Uncle."

Zion seemed too good to be true. I finally felt God heard my despair and sent me someone who could ease my pain and would be willing to help me out financially. However, my spirit, my intuition whatever you want to label it kept telling me all that glitters wasn't gold. I ignored the inclination because I desired a man at any costs. I wanted to be, no I needed to be in love.

One day I decided to use a half day of vacation and leave work early. I wasn't going to do anything in particular I just wanted some time for myself. I knew the house would be quiet and I could relax undisturbed from arguing children or a needy boyfriend. When I arrived home I was startled to see Zion's car in the driveway. I walked into the house but didn't find him downstairs.

I yelled a few times. "Zion, Zion."

I went upstairs, still no answer. I saw the bathroom door was partly opened. I slowly opened the door and found Zion sitting on the toilet, pants down around his ankles, a white substance around his nose, and on the upper portion of his lip. He was in a zone and didn't even acknowledge me standing there. .

"Zion."

He tilted his head toward the direction of my irritated voice. "Hey, baby. I didn't hear you come in. What are you doing home so early?"

"I could ask you the same question. Zion, what is that white stuff around your nose?"

He snickered, "Oh…that's just a little pick me up."

"A pick me up? What do you need that for?"

"Now Unique, all that good loving I put on you every night drains a brother. I need a little something, something to energize me."

I snatched the Zip Lock bag from the black and white marble bathroom sink. I waved it in the air.

"What is this Zion?"

"It's cocaine baby."

"Cocaine? Oh my, Lord. Zion, you can't snort cocaine in my house. Not around my kids. In fact I don't want any drugs in my home."

"Hold up girl. This is my house. I help pay the bills up in here."

"Zion, I know you are high because the deed of this house is only in my name! The little bit of money you give me doesn't even cover the electric bill. Once in awhile you do something extra. Now I understand why you're always broke. In the beginning of our relationship, you started off with all these grand gestures and helped out so much. I see now you were just a con. I was your mark so you could have someplace to stay in order for you to buy more drugs."

"All girl, don't complain. When I am giving you all this oversized meat and you start singing my name there's not a problem. Here try some. It will mellow you right on out."

"Are you serious right now? I don't want any of that poison! I'm going to lie down. You have given me a migraine."

"Hold up. I'll come with you."

"No, that won't be necessary. I only have a couple of hours to get some rest before the kids come home."

"Baby, that's all the time I need." Zion said as he flushed the toilet, washed his hands, and faced me as his muscular member stood at attention.

Before I knew it Zion was rocking me all over the bed. I screamed with ecstasy. After our fierce love making Zion admitted to me his cocaine habit was a daily ritual and he had been indulging in it for the last four years. He promised me the kids would never see the drugs or encounter him sniffing it up his nose. How did I allow myself to lower my standards? Was this relationship worth it? Where was my integrity? How could I kick him out when my body ached with pleasure? Satan had me in a vice and he knew I couldn't escape.

The kids were home from school. Marvin Gaye was playing on the record player signing "Got to give it up." I kept moving my head to beat of the music as I busily prepared a delicious meal in the oversized kitchen; spicy chili, rice, tossed salad, garlic bread, and freshly brewed iced tea.

I looked into the family room and watched them finish their homework assignments. Zion was helping Shannell with some math problems. I sipped on a glass of red wine. I felt good. I once again had a perfect family. The thought of possibly getting married for a second time crossed my mind. I never believed I could marry someone else but Zion was special. He was strong, sexy, easy on the eyes, and he loved my children like he was their biological father. I'm sure Grant would approve. I was startled from my trance when I heard Shannell speak.

"Uncle Zion."

"Yes sweetheart?"

"I have something in my eye. Can you get it out for me?"

"Sure, I can. Come stand in front of me."

Shannell bounced off of the couch and stood in front of him. Zion proceeded to position her in between his legs. The scene which unraveled before my eyes made my stomach turn. Vomit rose up and touched my tonsils. Zion grabbed Shannell's face and stroked her cheek gently. He looked in her eyes just like he did to me right before he penetrated me. Shannell was oblivious to the entire scenario which played before her.

I squealed, "Shannell, get away from Zion!"

"But Mommy, I have something in my eye."

"Shannell, do what I say right now! Move away! Clark, take your sisters and brother upstairs right this instance!"

"Mommy, my eye hurts."

"Shannell, Clark will take care of you. Just get out of here!"

The kids quickly departed from the family room. I listened for them as they climbed the stairs before I spoke to Zion.

"Damn, Unique, what the hell was that for? Why are you standing there looking at me all crazy? You seriously need to try some cocaine. You are so dramatic."

"Zion, I want you to pack your stuff and get out of my house, right now!"

"Girl you are tripping. I didn't do anything."

"Is that right? Then explain to me why you have a bulge in your pants? I saw how you looked at my baby, you drug infested pervert. Get the hell out, before I call the police on your ass!"

Zion rubbed his crotch. "I'll get out but don't call me when you need some money or when you need a fix from my rock! Yeah, your little girl looks real sweet. She's growing up real nice. Sweet, untouched, and pure nectar flowing from that fountain of youth not like your old stale ass."

I walked up to Zion and slapped him with every fiber of my being. My entire hand left an imprint along the right side of his face.

He instantaneously gripped my hand and raised his other hand to punch me. "Bitch, I'll kill you!"

"Stop it! You touch my Momma and I'm going to kill you!"

Simultaneously, we turned around to see an infuriated Clark holding one of Grant's old guns. I had forgotten we had it. I don't think there were any bullets in the gun but Zion didn't know any better.

Zion stuttered as he spoke. "Son, now son, you need, you need to put the gun down. You really, really don't want to shoot me. I'm practically your daddy."

"Liar! You'll never be my daddy! My mother asked you to leave. Now go upstairs, get your things, and never come back here."

At that moment, I saw the man Clark would become. In an instance he transformed into a resilient young man who looked out for his family. He was just like his daddy. I was so proud of him and yet so very scared.

Clark escorted Zion upstairs to our bedroom. He watched as Zion hurriedly packed his clothes. Without further incident, Clark walked Zion back down the stairs and out the front door.

I looked at my son. Contempt and anger were displayed in his eyes. "Clark, thank you. I know you shouldn't have to deal with this type of situation."

"Mom…as long as I live here, no other man will move into this home who is not married to you. You deserve better and so do we."

I couldn't believe my son had grown up right in front of my eyes. How did he get so wise? "Son, I am embarrassed. I promise you, this will never happen again. I…I don't know what has gotten into me. I've been so wrapped up in my own misery I haven't shown you and your siblings the right way to live. I have put all of you in danger with my selfish mistakes. Can you forgive your mother?"

Clark walked over to me, wrapped his sturdy arms around my waist, buried his face in my chest and cried. "I miss him too, Momma. We can't get him back but we can live. We can go on and make Daddy proud. He would want us to be happy. I love you Mom. I need you. We need you to come back to us."

Wow…out of the mouth of babes. Tears streamed from my swollen eyes. I hugged my son and kissed his tear streaked face. "Clark, I won't let you down ever again." We hugged and Clark went upstairs to check on his siblings.

The doorbell rang. "I know this fool didn't come back!" Without looking to see who was at the door I snatched it open and precipitously stepped back.

"Oh…I thought you were someone else."

"I'm sorry to intrude, Mrs. Johnson. I know the hour is late. I usually don't make house calls."

"How do you know who I am? Who are you and what do you want?

"Pardon me. Where are my manners? Mrs. Johnson, my name is Angel Mercy. I am the proprietor of A.M. Jewelers located downtown at the U.S. Steel Tower on Grant Street. May I come in?"

I was startled but I wasn't afraid of this angelic looking white man.

"I don't understand. I've never been to your store. How do you know me?"

Mr. Mercy stood in the doorway waiting for his invitation to enter. Out of know where a brisk gust of wind swept through the doorway and chilled us both.

"Your husband Grant…"

"You must be mistaken my husband is dead."

"I know Mrs. Johnson. Please can I come in? I promise to explain everything."

"Of course you can."

We both dispensed a nervous chuckle as I ushered Mr. Mercy into the living room. For some reason I started to feel calm deep down on the inside. A peace which surpassed all understanding was invading my insides and the atmosphere in my home seemed to shift. It was something I hadn't felt in years. A serene spirit started to fill the air and engulfed our presence.

"Mrs. Johnson, as I was saying your husband used to come in my store all of the time. Judge Houston's office is a few floors above my store."

A slight twinge of mortification crept up my back at the mention of the Judge's name.

"Grant, came to your store? Why?'

"I used to look forward to his visits. He had such zeal for life. Grant wanted to purchase a special gift for you. He told me when you first got married he promised to get you a ten karat diamond engagement ring. He was disappointed he didn't get to play professional basketball but he loved his life. He said God had abundantly blessed him. He was proud of his family. He couldn't stop saying how much he loved you. It was such a joy to hear about true love."

Remembering my wedding day brought tears of joy. I was so in love with him, I thought our love would never end.

"I'm sorry, Mrs. Johnson. I didn't mean to cause you any pain."

"Oh, no Mr. Mercy, for the first time in years these are tears of joyfulness. I haven't thought about my wedding day since my husband died."

"I am glad you are healing. You know God has been with you. He has seen your pain and late in the midnight hour He heard your cries. I apologize, when I think of God's goodness I get off track. I just want to tell everybody about Him. Anyway, I was cleaning out my safe and way in the back was this box wrapped in a note. I couldn't believe it. After all these years, I never realized it was still in there. We 've conducted numerous inventories and cleaned out the safe but somehow it was overlooked."

"What, a box with a note, for me?"

"Yes, my dear. For several years, before your husband's untimely death he was making bi-monthly installments for your gift. I usually don't extend credit for such a long time but Grant seemed like an extraordinary exceptional young family man who loved you but more importantly he loved The Lord. He still owed me some money but sometimes it's not about the money. So, I'm here to make a special delivery. Please take this box and note. Miss Unique, it has been an honor to finally meet you. I feel like I have known you forever. I shall leave you now."

I was stunned. I couldn't believe I held the last gift and note from Grant. This was such an unexpected treasure. I watched the fragile Mr. Mercy put on his oversized white coat. He walked toward the door, turned in my direction and smiled as his eyes sparkled with pure delight.

"You know, Unique your mother gave you the perfect name because you were uniquely made and you have a unique purpose for this day and time."

This gentile man was not making any sense but I just nodded in agreement. I was really ready for him to leave.

"Mr. Mercy, are sure I can't pay you the balance?"

He waved his hand in the air, "No, no, it's not necessary, my dear. Consider it a gift from above. He has a strange way of working things out. You know our God is always right on time, never late and He has preordained our destiny. Stay focused my child your breakthrough is on the horizon. Your setback was only temporary. Your comeback will far exceed anything your mind can conceive or achieve on your own. God is about to elevate you to the next level. He has always loved you. He is all you've ever needed. Grant's love, the love of your children or friends cannot compare to the love our Father has bestowed on you. Remember, there is nothing and I mean nothing you have done that God is not willing to forgive. If you just repent, turn from your wicked ways and accept Him into your life. Surrender all and be blessed."

Whoa…that was a lot for my mind to handle. Without another word Angel Mercy exited my home as quickly as he had entered. I don't know what happened but I began to feel all of my heavy laden burdens being lifted. I felt an earthshattering supernatural joy bubbling deep down in my insides.

My hands trembled as I held the beautiful purple leather box trimmed with gold. The note addressed on white parchment was indeed penned by Grant. He had excellent penmanship. I knew his handwriting anywhere. My heart delighted as I reminisced about the love letters he often left me when he went to school or work.

Hours passed as I praised God, repented, asked Him to strengthen me and to deliver me out of the wilderness. I hadn't gone before The Lord in years. I was worn out with my private praise party, just Jesus and me. It was then I felt empowered enough to open the note. I sensed Grant's spirit as I read his final words to me.

"Dear Unique,

It's been a long time and often a struggle but worth every penny I have put on this gift. All the years of overtime I worked and the sacrificed time away from you and the kids made my commitment to you a reality. I love you deep down in the depths of my soul. Even as a kid I believed in destiny. I knew from the moment I first laid eyes on you, I loved you and we were meant to be together. I knew you would be the mother of my children. You are the greatest! You are my best friend, my support, my lover, my wife. Our love is a love of a lifetime and will last forever. Enjoy this token of my sincerest appreciation and gratitude for all you have done in our family's life. Our children are beyond blessed to have a dedicated mother like you. You always put our needs before yourself and I love you for your unselfishness. When you wear this token of my gratefulness I know it will bring a smile across your face and you will always think of me. I will always be with you. I'll love you today, tomorrow, a month from now and even years from now. God has imprinted you in my heart. I will always be your one true love, Grant.

P.S. I delivered on my promise and then some. Count them…twelve carats, baby!"

Oh… Jesus, Grant would be ashamed of the woman I've become and how our children were at times neglected. Did he know the void he left in my life? Would he have forgiven me?

My hands shook frenziedly. My heart pounded and pulsated in my ears. I could barely open the box. Unexpectedly, the lid popped open. Whew! There it sparkled, the most beautiful, brilliant, solitary, princess cut diamond. It was accentuated with three rows of diamonds which wrapped all away around to back of the ring. It was simply amazing. I slipped on the ring and placed it on top of my wedding band. It fit perfectly. Instantly, I felt totally whole.

I climbed into bed and retrieved my journal out of the nightstand drawer. I hadn't written in it since I buried Grant but tonight I truly felt God's presence. It seemed this stranger, Angel Mercy during our brief visit breathed fresh life into my home and my heart.

I began to write; "I was shattered, broken, filled with despair and drowning in my transgressions. I could not face another day with the shackles of life which weighed me down and had me bound. I cried and cried but no one heard me then I remembered your name, Jesus. I whispered Jesus, one night as my soul was dying. You heard me and breathed life into my spirit, renewed my mind, and gave me purpose.

No longer did my transgressions haunt me. Oh yes, I was reborn with just a whisper of your name, Jesus, my shattered broken life rebirthed. Jesus, you set me free to be used for your honor and glory. Jesus, you gave me clarity."

I drifted off to sleep and for the first time since Grant's death I slept peacefully and didn't have any nightmares. Instead, the nightmares were replaced with all the great moments we shared.

I visualized I saw Grant. He sat on a mountain top as the clouds hovered slightly above him. The sky was a stunning shade of baby blue. From his perch he watched over our home which sat in a deep valley. Clothed in white he looked handsome and radiant. He was surrounded by a majestically bright aura. There was no doubt he was a child of the King. Marvelous, magnificent, white, bellowing wings were anchored at his side and had an expansive twelve foot span. I was standing in our backyard looking up toward the mountain. The glare from the sun slightly blinded me as I watched him descended from the mountain and float toward me. He picked me up, twirled me around. We floated in the air as our bodies entwined and rhythmically danced with a melody only our hearts knew. Then he draped his gigantic wings around us and hugged me for the last time. I nuzzled my face in the crook of his neck and placed my mouth next to his ear and said, "Thank you." A single tear dropped from his eye. He didn't utter a word as he placed my feet back on solid ground. He flashed his glorious smile, nodded, outstretched his wings and ascended into the clouds.

As I slept, God spoke to my spirit. I heard him whisper, "Surrender all and be blessed."

Chapter 25

I woke up the next morning renewed, refreshed and rejuvenated. I had a new walk. There was a new pep in my step. I couldn't wait to call Netta. I had to tell her about Angel Mercy, my gift from Grant, my dream, and most importantly my rebirth. I was reborn with God's love instilled in me and with a promise to fulfill my purpose, my destiny.

I grabbed my journal for a second time because God was speaking to me. I was in awe of my apparent overnight transformation. I felt like the lady with the issue of blood. All she wanted was just a touch of the Master even if it was the hem of His garment and when she touched Him she was instantly healed of her affliction. I had been healed of my demonic influences. Lust, sexual perversion, depression, and suicidal thoughts had left me because I called on Jesus.

I sipped on my hot chocolate and penned my poem. The words effortlessly flowed out me like the downpour of rain as it saturated a barren field in order for new life to spring forth and bear fruit. I had been washed by the rain and given a second chance. I had to call Netta.

I was so excited my fingers were discombobulated as I dialed Netta. She answered on the third ring.

"Hello, Netta."

"Good morning, Unique. What has you up so early on this beautiful Sunday?"

"Well, I've encountered the presence of God. I called to tell you I'm going to be alright."

"Hallelujah! Hallelujah! Hallelujah! She shouted through the phone.

I continued to tell her of how God spoke to my spirit and how I knew Grant was okay and would always watch over us. I told her everything. When I finished telling her my experience all Netta could say was "Hallelujah. God answered my prayers."

"Netta, do you have a few moments? I want to share with you what the Holy Ghost placed in my heart."

"Honey, after what you told me, I have all the time in the world."

"Great. Well, it's called Your Struggle."

"I'm ready to hear what the good Lord has done. Come on with it."

"Okay…here it goes. Your struggle is your foundation which I can build upon to make you stand against the storms and tell them to move.

My word declares I shall never leave or forsake you, so struggle on.

You can't see my divine plan but know it has already been set into motion, so struggle on.

Your cross may seem too heavy to carry but know I am holding up your arms and moving your feet toward great destiny, so struggle on.

You may not see my master plan but it will manifest itself daily if you just stay strong, be faithful and struggle on.

Struggle on my dear child, for what is ahead, promises to be better than yesterday. Your pain and sorrow has not gone unnoticed so struggle on to your great reward.

And when the struggle is over and you look back over your life, your struggle will be a distant memory but one which you can reflect on every now and again just in case you forget who I am and what I did for you, so struggle on.

And now My work is done as the struggle has strengthened your character, given you power, unshakeable faith, and has cemented your spirit with a solid foundation so you can soar through the storms and tell them to move with all power and might in your hand.

S- standing in front of the storm and

T - trusting it will be over soon, as you

R- remain steadfast with your face set like a flint

U- until His master plan manifest's in your life in order to

G- guide you toward your divine purpose and to prepare you to call on

G- God for He shall supply all of your needs and to

L- lean on His grace and mercy

E- exalting His name forever and ever."

Loud uncontrollable sobbing came from the other end of the phone line. "Netta, Netta, are you alright? Don't you like it?"

"Yes, I'm fine. I love it! God's glory is all over you. I knew you had a prophetic word in you all along you just had to bind the hands of the devil. Look at what He has done for you in less than twenty-four hours. Prayer works. Today is the first day of the rest of your life."

"Thank you, Netta. I have never been so excited nor did I expect God to do something for me but it's time for a change. I have tried everything and everybody. Now it's time to try His way and His will for my life. Nothing I have done on my own has worked. He is my only hope."

"Unique, He's all you have ever needed. Now surrender and be blessed."

"Oh…my goodness Netta, that's what Angel Mercy told me and God whispered it in my ear."

"Sounds to me, you just got confirmation. Unique, I have to get ready for church."

"What time does church start?" I asked Netta. There was dead silence.

"Hello…Netta?"

Then I heard shouting. "Thank you Jesus! Thank you Lord. Hallelujah! The prayers of the righteous have been answered. My God you are good!"

Her praise went on for a good ten minutes. "Um…Netta, what time is church? We are going to be late."

"Ten o'clock. I'll see you soon. I have to get off this phone, get dressed and praise the Lord."

"Okay, Netta. I love you."

"I love you too."

"Netta…wait."

"Yes, my darling?"

"I just want to thank you."

"Thank me for what? I didn't do anything special."

"Oh…Netta, you have been my rock and you never gave up on me. Thank you for praying for me when I couldn't pray for myself. Thank you for loving me when I was in the midst of all my mess."

"Oh Unique, you are my dear, dear sweet child." Netta said through her tears. "I loved you because He loved you first. I knew my God was bigger than your mess. I knew you had to go through your trials and tribulations so you could be a testimony for someone else. My Lord, child, get ready because He is going to use you in a powerful way. Your life is about to change. Hallelujah! See you at church."

"Bye, Netta."

I hung up the phone from Netta. I got on my knees to pray. I thanked God for Netta, my children, Ruby, Char, Mrs. Johnson, and the triplets. I thanked God for forgiving and loving me even when I didn't love myself."

Chapter 26

After a few months of going to church, Bible Study, Sunday school, choir practice and anything else I could do to stay in God's presence I did it. The more I sought God and began to seek a personal relationship with him the more I began to hear his voice and receive revelation concerning the next chapter of my life.

Netta almost died from her happiness as my entire family accepted Jesus Christ as our Lord and Savior.

Since my resurrection, so to speak, it seemed late in the midnight hour God always had a word for me. Maybe, that's because it was the only time I was still and free from distractions. When I awakened, it was impressed in my heart I should go to college and get a business degree. I spoke with Netta and she agreed to watch the children while I attended school at night.

Her exact words were, "If I could watch them while you were out in the world screwing all those men, then I can certainly watch them, when you are trying to live right." Only Netta could tell me exactly how she was feeling.

I graduated with a B. S. degree in Business Management from the University of Pittsburgh and continued my educational endeavors by earning a Master's of Business Administration. Netta and the kids were in attendance for my big day. It was a long struggle but I persevered. My family beamed with pride. They loudly chanted my name as I walked the platform to receive my diploma. Afterwards, they waited for me outside of the auditorium. Their arms were filled with flowers, balloons and candy.

Dinner at the Cheesecake Factory was delicious. The Cajun Jambalaya Pasta was scrumptious. I thought I was going to burst but I still managed to save room for the Mango Key Lime cheesecake. At dinner I told Netta of my plans to open a facility for women who needed second chances. I told her about the concept concerning Visions of Beauty. She was thrilled.

"Unique, dear, do you have a location in mind? Are you going to build from scratch and more importantly where in the world are you going to get the money?"

"Honestly, Netta, I don't know but I do know God doesn't give you vision without provision. I have no doubt this plan will come to fruition."

"Well, praise God. I believe. Look, dear it's been a long day. These old bones are tiered. It's way past my bedtime. I'm going on home. Love you."

"Love you too, Netta. Thanks for being by my side."

"Child, where else would I be?"

We chuckled and kissed each other on the cheek and said our goodbyes. She hugged the kids and left the restaurant.

By the time we got home it was almost ten. The kids went straight to bed. Before I retired for the night, I lingered around the family room and opened up some mail. I noticed the flashing red light on the answering machine. I pushed the play button and was horrified by the voice which vibrated out from the recording.

"Unique, this is Randall. Randall Houston. It is imperative that I see you tomorrow at noon at my downtown office. I promise not to take too much of your time. Please come."

The message ended. The nerve of that perverted old b…calling me after all of these years. I wasn't going to give him a second thought but I felt a sense of urgency in my spirit to keep the appointment.

Chapter 27

It was 11:55 a.m. when I arrived on the sixth floor of the US Steel building. Judge Houston's office was to the left of the bank of elevators. His office was modest to say the least. You wouldn't know he had such a long and prestigious career.

I walked into the office but no secretary was behind the huge gray and green marble desk.

"Hello, is anyone here?"

A frail and aging Judge Houston appeared from the oval door.

"Unique, thank you for honoring my request," he said as he ushered me inside his office. He motioned for me to sit in the leather chair that was positioned in front of his dilapidated desk.

"Judge Houston, please tell me why after all of these years, have you summoned me to your office? I'm sure whatever you have to say could have been done via telephone."

He shifted in his seat. "You're mistaken, Unique, it's imperative what I need to say, is said in person."

I was annoyed. "Go ahead, Judge, I'm listening."

"First, I owe you an apology. I had no right to take advantage of you so many years ago. It has haunted me every day since then but I was a coward and didn't have the courage until now to apologize."

"Why, now, what has changed?"

"I have stage four lung cancer. It has spread to other organs and my lymph nodes. I'm afraid I don't have much time left. I wanted to make amends to those I have hurt by my unwarranted actions."

I could see the sincerity in his eyes.

"I'm sorry to hear this, Judge. I pray you are not in a great deal of pain."

"You're a kind soul, Unique. I appreciate your kindheartedness and concern. Thank you. The pain it's manageable so I won't complain. I suppose I won't get any peace until I close my eyes for the final time. I beg you to forgive me. I undeniably had no right to violate you or Grant's memory. He was like a son to me. I'm ashamed of my behavior. Can you find it in your heart to grant a dying man's wish of forgiveness?"

I got up from the chair and moved toward Judge Houston. I placed is feeble hand in mine.

"Judge Houston, he who is without sin can cast the first stone. I forgive you as Christ has forgiven me."

I hugged the skin and bones of the once distinguished Judge Randall Houston. Tears spilled down his face.

"Thank you, Unique. I pray I can get into heaven. I've scorned, dishonored, and trampled on a lot of people in my lifetime to get the career I wanted. Unfortunately, I'm afraid I have numerous enemies and not enough time to apologize."

I returned to my seat. "Judge, if you are truly sorrowful, I believe by God's grace and mercy He will forgive you. I pray your soul will rest in eternal peace. I should be leaving now."

"Wait, I have a graduation present for you."

"What? How did you know I graduated?"

"I may be dying but I'm not dead yet. I still have influence and people who report to me. I've been watching you from afar. You should be proud of your accomplishments. Here take this."

He reached into the inside pocket of his blue sports coat. He handed me an envelope.

"Please, open it."

I proceeded to rip open the envelope and pulled out a check. My mouth dropped. Surely, my eyes were deceiving me. It was a check for two hundred and fifty thousand dollars.

"Judge Houston, I…I can't accept this. It's too much."

"Please Unique, take it. I promise you, there are no strings attached. I don't have any family. The majority of my finances have been divided between various organizations. You would honor me by taking this money and do something with it which will help others. I have tried my entire life to serve the people of this great city. That's all I ask for you in return."

"I'm stunned. Are you sure about this?"

"Yes, Unique, I'm one hundred percent sure. I'm afraid I must cut our meeting short. I'm due in Squirrel Hill for an appointment. I'll see you to the elevator."

The doors of the elevator opened. Before I walked onto the elevator I hugged him and wished him well. That was the last time I saw Judge Randall Houston. He died a week later.

On my way out of the building the elevator stopped on the fourth floor and to my surprise Angel Mercy walked on. It had been such a long time since his brief visit at my home but I never could forget him or the night my life changed.

Gleefully, I spoke, "Mr. Mercy, it's so good to see you."

"Unique, what a surprise to see you here, you still look stunning. By the way, I understand congratulations are in order. You should be very proud of all your endeavors. You have done quite well for yourself."

Stunned, twice in one day was a bit much. "How did you know?"

"Oh, I have connections. If you have a moment, please join me, at the store. I'll order lunch and we can catch up with all the things that are happening in your life. I would love to hear every detail."

"Sure, why not but please don't order me any lunch. It's getting late, I can hold out for dinner."

"Okay, very well, my dear."

We got off the elevator on the second floor and entered the most exquisite jewelry store I'd ever seen. We chatted for hours. I told him about Visions of Beauty and he was overjoyed with my plans.

"Unique, have you scouted out any localities?"

"Oh, no Angel, this project is in its infancy stages. I have to crawl before I can walk."

"I disagree. Some people skip crawling altogether. I believe you are going to be a sprinter. You are on a mission, no time for baby steps or Similac."

"Well, actually I do like the North Side."

"Unique, if you don't mind, let's call my son Moses. I believe he could be a valuable asset to this project. He's a real estate investor and an architect."

"Oh, yes, please call him but I'm not sure I can afford his services."

"At the moment, let's not worry about finances. Excuse me while I give him a call."

I browsed around Angele's exquisite store and admired much of the jewelry as I waited for him to return from his phone call.

"Good news, Unique, my son is actually on the North Side. Do you know where the Alleghany Commons is at?"

"Yes, I do."

"Great, he will be waiting for you. You should leave now in order to miss the rush hour traffic."

"How will I know him?"

"You'll know him because he will probably be in one of his fancy cars."

"Oh…okay. Thank you so much Angel. I am very happy I ran into you."

"The pleasure has been all mine, I'll see you again. Bless you, my dear. I look forward to watching what else God has in store for you."

I made it to Alleghany Commons in record time. I pulled behind a red Corvette and exited my car. A well-dressed, distinguished looking African American man, probably in his mid-fifties with gray right around the edges of his temples emerged from the vehicle.

"Well, this certainly isn't Angel's son." I mumbled to myself.

"Miss Johnson?"

Apprehensively, I acknowledged him, "Yes, I'm Mrs. Johnson."

He smiled and extended his hand. I'm Angel's son, Moses Abraham."

I stood there in shock.

He chuckled, "I know, I get that look all the time. Angel is my adoptive father."

"Oh, I apologize for being startled I just wasn't expecting a… a black man."

"No, problem, I understand. So let's try this again."

"Mrs. Johnson, I'm Moses Abraham and it is a pleasure to meet you. My father speaks very highly of you."

I extended my hand, "It's nice to meet you, Mr. Abraham."

"Please, call me Moses."

"Only, if you call me, Unique."

"Deal," we said in unison.

"My dad tells me you want to build a center to empower women who have or are going through struggles. Come, and walk with me. I want to show you something."

We walked together and crossed the street.

"Yes, I am looking at to build a facility that has many components which can facilitate the all-around well-being; mental, physical, and spiritual aspects of women who have been wounded by life's circumstances. Like one stop shopping for the cultivation and renewing of your soul. I haven't worked out all the particulars but I am getting it together."

"I'm very impressed. I admire your tenacity and your drive to succeed. I believe in giving back and helping others. My father instilled that in me from a very young age. It's a part of my spiritual DNA."

We stopped walking in front of a large corner plot of land.

"Well, we've arrived at our destination."

"Here, at this desolate piece of land? I don't understand."

"My father and I purchased this property about twenty-five years ago for a very reasonable price. We never could decide what we wanted to do with it that is until today."

"I'm sorry, Moses. I'm not following you."

"Unique, we would like to sell you this land in order for you to build your business."

I was stunned for the third time today. "I…I don't know what to say."

"It's simple, just say yes. You know it's getting chilly. Follow me to Pirmanti Brother's so we can further discuss the details."

I could barely speak, "Alright."

I followed behind Moses in his high-class vehicle. We arrived at the restaurant right before the dinner crowd descended on Pittsburgh's legendary eatery. Since 1933 Pirmanti Brother's served the best corned beef and pastrami sandwiches in the world and had been featured on many national television shows. My mouth watered just thinking about eating one of the delectable treasures.

We were seated at a corner table near the entrance. The waitress quickly placed our menus in front of us and departed. She returned momentarily and took our drink orders.

"So, Unique, since you haven't looked at the menu I am going to assume you know what you want to order. Let me guess… a corn beef sandwich on rye, brown mustard, lettuce, pickles, and provolone cheese."

I broke out with laughter, "Why, Moses how do you know me so well? You were almost correct."

He raised his left eyebrow, "Really? So what did I get wrong?"

"I'll have wheat bread instead of rye. And you?"

"I'll have the same."

Moses motioned for the waitress who eagerly took our orders.

I took a sip of my water. "Moses, you really took me by surprise. I can't believe you want me to buy your land. It's so generous of you. Unfortunately, there is no way I can afford it. My credit isn't in the best standings and I'm positive I can't secure a bank loan. Therefore, I must respectively decline the offer."

"Unique, I haven't given you a price. You need to hear me out first."

"Okay, but…"

"Look, I'm a single middle-aged man who has done very well. I've been looking for a way to give back on a grander scale. My father and I would like to sell you the land for two hundred and fifty thousand dollars. It's what we originally paid for it."

I was drinking my water when the glass automatically left my hand and crashed to the floor as I grabbed my chest. I felt flushed. The waitress ran over to us and proceeded to clean up the shards of glass.

"Unique, are you okay? You don't look well."

I wiped the sweat from my brow. "Sweet Jesus, I'm…I'm just amazed at what God is doing. Did you really say two hundred and fifty thousand dollars?"

"Yes, I did. If it's too much I know we can work out some type of arrangement. I really believe in you."

My heart was palpitating at an unusually rapid pace. I could barely catch my breath.

"No, it's fine. You, don't understand. Before I saw your father I was given that exact amount as a gift. I have it right here in my purse."

Moses leaned back in his chair and winked. "Well, look at God. He does work in mysterious ways. So are you going to accept my offer?"

"Yes, of course. Moses, I accept. I can endorse the check over to you right now. I can't thank you and your father enough. This is a dream coming true."

"Fantastic! Can you meet me in the morning at the bank around nine? We can transfer the money, the deed and get this project started."

"I will be there at 8:45 blowing a trumpet."

We laughed.

Our food arrived and we temporarily ate in silence.

"Unique, now that you have a place to build I would like to offer you something else."

"Moses, I don't think my heart can take any more excitement."

"I want to give you my architectural services. Design your facility, take care of the contractors and get you up and running."

"Moses, my Lord, this is beyond a liberal offer but I can't afford you. It was by God's grace I had the money to procure the land."

"Unique, let me tell you something, when I was twelve, Angel Mercy rescued me from slanging drugs on the corner. I was the typical statistic. My mother died from a drug overdose and my father was one of her no name johns. I raised myself by living anywhere I could and I ate whatever leftovers someone discarded.

I had the faith of a mustard seed and I told God while I was sleeping on a cardboard box in some alley, if you deliver me from this hell I will serve you all the days of my life. You know what? He heard me by sending me this frail white man who happened to be driving on the wrong side of town at the right time. Angel took me in. He never judged me about my past. Instead he nurtured me, sent me to the best schools and gave me unconditional love. He was and is my answered prayer.

If you allow me to help you, I will be giving back as I believe God would want me to aide you in fulfilling your dream. You see there is no coincidence. This is divine favor working in your life."

"For once, I am at a loss for words. Hallelujah! I will gladly accept your services but I have to pay you back."

"Okay, since you insist how about this… one year from the day you open the doors to Visions of Beauty you can start repaying me. We will come up with a reasonable payment at a later date. Does that sound fair?"

"Moses Abraham, you got yourself a deal. Let's drink to that."

We clanked our water glasses together and shook hands. Five hours later we were closing down the restaurant. We talked like we had known each other our entire lives. I truly had a good time. He walked me to my car.

"Unique, I have immensely enjoyed your company. I would like to do this again if you don't mind?"

"I had a great time. I can't remember the last time I laughed so much and spilled my life story to someone other than my best friends. Yes, I would like to have dinner with you again."

We made it to my car and he opened the door for me. "I'll see you tomorrow morning at the bank at nine. Don't be late."

"I promise, I won't be late, you have a good evening, Mr. Moses."

"Trust me I will sleep like a baby."

He winked, closed my car door, and I drove off. For the first time in decades I enjoyed another man's company and sex didn't even enter my mind. A platonic, refreshing friendship with a man is what I had been missing.

Chapter 28

For almost two and a half years, I was consumed day and night with blue prints, paint colors, tile, sound systems, hair dryers, furniture, pews, gym equipment, and Moses Abraham. He had become an intercut part of my life and the development of Visions of Beauty. His tutelage was invaluable. He made me feel alive and we hadn't even shared a kiss. It was true joy to know each other intimately without the distractions of an overrated sex life.

I'm not going to lie I wanted him and I'm sure he wanted me but we had to put God first so everything else would follow. It had been a long time but I was loving life.

We had a meeting at the site and to my surprise there was Angel.

"Unique, it is good to see you this morning, looking radiant as always. Doesn't she look good, son?"

I blushed at the compliment.

"Yes, Father. She always looks like a ray of sunshine."

"Please, gentlemen. Enough already, I thank you. Angel it's always nice to see you. So what brings you by this morning?"

"Well, I wanted to see what you have done with the building and I know it is about eighty-five percent completed. Moses told me you are waiting to build the sanctuary."

"Yes, that's true. I want to make sure we get the space consecrated unto the Lord and that it is built flawlessly. I want women to be able to lie in front of the Lord and receive deliverance."

Angel nodded. "I couldn't agree with you more which brings me to this visit."

"Go ahead, Father tell her." Moses said impatiently.

"Patience is a virtue my son, patience."

"Yes, sir, I apologize."

I wanted to laugh at the little boy which just appeared out of this mid-fifties man as he was corrected by his Father.

"As I was saying, I agree the church should be the core of your facility and I want to ensure it is equipped with everything. So I am donating one million dollars."

"Angel, no, that's too much. I can't."

Moses was shaking his head no in my direction as to not argue with his dad.

"I insist and this is a donation. There is no repayment but to honor the will of God."

"Angel, I'm overwhelmed by your family's generosity. I don't deserve such kindness."

Moses stepped in. "Why not, Unique? Why do you still think you deserve less? There is no condemnation here. Your past has been forgiven and it does not define or hinder your future. You learn from it, let it build your character, leave it, and move on. So you deserve all the blessings. Don't ever forget that."

I somberly shook my head as I was still learning about correction. Angel broke the awkward silence.

"Well, I'm off. I can't wait for the grand opening. He is pleased with your works."

Angel kissed me on the check and hugged his son and quickly exited the building.

I looked at Moses. "I am trying to get better about the blessings I deserve. I just have flashbacks sometimes of the things I've done. I'm ashamed."

Moses grabbed my hand and gently rubbed my cheek. "Honey, let it go. It has been cast into the sea of forgiveness never to be picked up again. But I do believe you need to let go of something."

"What is it?"

"You need to take off your wedding rings. I'm not trying to be insensitive but it has been decades since Grant died and yet you still wear his rings. It's time to let him go and move on."

"Moses, he will always be a part of me because he is in my children."

"I understand. Truly, I do but you are holding onto a past, which will never be resurrected. I know you love your ring. If you have to wear it, why don't you wear it on your right hand? And your wedding band can be kept in a jewelry box. You know my father has some gorgeous jewelry boxes. I'm sure he would be more than happy to have one custom made for you."

I was taken aback. I was hurt and angry. Who did Moses Abraham think he was to tell me what I should do with my wedding rings? He had some nerve. I walked away from him.

He called after me, "Unique."

I didn't speak to him for two days. He showed up at my house unannounced. Lorna answered the door and yelled upstairs.

"Momma, Mr. Abraham is here to see you."

I started to walk down the stairs and I heard Lorna and Moses.

"Thank you, Lorna. How is school?"

"This last year of high school is a breeze. I took all of my harder courses last year. I can't wait to go to Spelman and walk in my mother's shoes."

I busted in on the conversation, "And I can't wait to have the house all to myself."

All of us laughed.

"She's going to miss me, Mr. Abraham. She's just putting up a good front."

"I agree, Lorna. She will be crying like a baby."

"See you later Mom. I'm going bowling with Jenna. Bye, Mr. Abraham."

"Good bye", we said in unison.

I observed the rejected looking Moses and noticed a bouquet of red roses in his hand.

"Are those for me?"

"Yes, it's a peace offering. I've missed you and I'm so sorry if I offended you. That was not my intention."

I didn't respond right away. Instead, I momentarily left him standing in the living room as I entered the kitchen and retrieved a vase from underneath the kitchen sink. I returned with the beautiful flowers in the container and sat them on the dining room table.

He followed me into the family room. We sat on the couch and I muted the Steelers game.

"Moses, I accept your apology but you were right. I was holding on and continuing to give life to a dead situation. Look, do you see something different?"

I flashed him my hands. He looked flabbergasted.

"You took your rings off and moved the engagement ring to your right hand. Where is your band?"

"As you suggested your father had the perfect jewelry box."

"How do you feel about this new transition?"

"Oddly, Moses, I feel free. It's time to embrace all of my future."

Moses looked intently in my eyes. He leaned in closer and our lips met. He was gentle and yet so electrifying. The kiss left me breathless and exhilarated. He suddenly pulled away.

"Unique, I'm sorry. I…"

"It's alright Moses. We have been waiting a long time for this moment. I'm sorry it took me so long to follow my heart."

"You never need to apologize to me, Unique. You mean the world to me. I love you."

"You what?"

"I said, I love you, I have loved you from the first day I saw you."

Wow! Talk about Déjà vu. I had heard those words before. Was Grant telling me it was okay to be in love again?

"I love you too. Moses, you have made me whole and encouraged me. These past two and a half years have restored my joy."

"Destiny is always a journey and I'm grateful God saw fit to put us together. You are truly unique, Miss Unique Johnson."

"Yes, I am. You see God made me unique right from the start. Well… that's what Momma told me."

Prologue

"Momma, hurry up. We are going to be late." Isaiah shouted from the bottom of the stairs.

"I'm coming." I said as I slipped on my black and gold stilettos.

"You look beautiful, Mom. I'm so proud of you."

"Thank you, son, where are your sisters and brother?"

"Oh…they went to pick up Netta. They will meet us at the ceremony. Clark put me in charge of getting you there on time. If we don't hurry he is going to whip my behind. You know he thinks he's our daddy."

We cracked up laughing.

I looked in the mirror for one last look over. "Come on, boy. I'm ready."

We headed out the door. "Wait!" I screamed, "I forgot my speech on the table."

"I got it mom. You really need to relax. This day has been a long time coming. It's in God's hands."

"I know son but I am a ball of nerves."

"Mom, surrender all and be blessed. Enjoy this day."

We rode the rest of the way in silence. Isaiah was right. This grand opening had been a long time coming and a wonderful journey. The Mayor, the Governor along with the press including Pratt Wilson would be in attendance. This was an event not to be missed. Anybody that thought they were somebody wanted to be seen at the grand opening.

When we pulled up to the building a red carpet was stretched in front of the doorway. A huge red ribbon was attached to the entrance waiting for me to officially cut it off and open the doors to Visions of Beauty. It was a spectacular site. Moses had done an exceptional job with the layout and planning of the building. The landscape was immaculate. The building was in pristine shape.

Moses came and escorted me out of the car and led me to the podium. My family, Netta and Angel were all sitting in the stand beaming with pride. It was finally my moment.

My black "v" neck dress clung to all my curves. My wide brimmed asymmetrical black and gold hat accentuated my outfit.

Moses stepped to the podium and a hush fell upon the crowd.

"I like to call Pastor Rollins to the stand."

"Good Afternoon Everyone, It is my pleasure and an honor to be here today to bless this unique facility. I have known Unique since she was a child and she has grown into an incredible women. She is a testimony that you should never let your trials and tribulations derail you from your destiny. God will use you right where you are. Your past does not predict your future. Your past is your training ground for God to prune and mold you into who He wants you to be. Can I get an Amen?"

The crowd shouted, "Amen."

"Father, in the name of Jesus we humbly come before you giving you thanks for this facility. Thank you for Unique Johnson, for her obedience and willingness to be used by You. Bless her in everything that she touches. Bless and cover her children and her children's children and all the generations to come. We ask that you cover this place with the precious blood of your Son. We thank you for your Word that says no weapons formed against us shall prosper and we believe this place will be a safe haven and a refuge for women to get beautified from the inside out. Bless all those abundantly who had a helping hand in bringing this facility to our great city. We thank you for what you have done, we thank you for what you are doing now, and we thank you for what you are about to do in Jesus name. Let the people say Amen."

Once again with a thunderous applause the crowd shouted, "Amen."

Moses walked up to Pastor Rollins, gave him a hug, and removed the microphone from his hand.

"Ladies and gentlemen, it gives me great pleasure to introduce to you the lady of the hour, the visionary behind Visions of Beauty, Miss Unique Blackman Johnson."

I received a standing ovation. I could not believe the sea of people who surrounded the building. I stood briefly in awe before I spoke. Then unexpected tears flowed as I looked out at the crowd and there stood Ruby and Char. They waved and blew me kisses. I had no idea they were there. What a surprise. I tried to compose myself. Moses handed me a handkerchief.

"Thank you. Thank you. Please be seated."

Slowly the applause dissipated and the audience took their seats.

"First, I like to thank God who is the head of my life. I'd like to thank Mayor Dixon, Governor Hawkins and all the distinguished guests who have gathered here today. My heart is full and in awe of what God has done.

I'd like to thank Netta Peters for standing by me through the most difficult times of my life. Ruby and Char my childhood friends who have been with me through the good, the bad, and the ugly. To Moses Abraham and Angel Mercy my true angels here on earth who were instrumental in bringing this vision to light. I can't thank you enough for what you have done for me. Lastly, but not least I like to thank my four incredible children, Clark, Shannell, Isaiah, and Lorna. You are the reason for my being. I am honored God chose me to be your mother. I have been truly blessed to watch you grow into wonderful, responsible, caring, loving young adults. I am proud of each of you and love you with all my heart.

Today we cut this ribbon on your legacy. Today I let all of you know with Christ all things are possible. We are all here because of those who have gone before us and paved the way for such a time as this. I wrote this poem, Our History is Rich in honor of the people who have left us a rich inheritance.

Our history is rich like a finely woven tapestry each thread made stronger by the thread before. The ties that bind us make our history unique. We are a race of people who have endured generations after generations of hatred, injustices, heartache, and pain yet we have survived it all. We are a strong people who have persevered and triumphed through all adversities for we stand on the shoulders of our ancestors. We are a diverse people who come in many shapes, sizes, and beautiful colors. Our history is rich.

From the slave ships in chains traveling through the Middle Passage to the Underground Railroad to the steps of the White House, our history is rich.

From Sojourner Truth to Harriet Tubman, Frederick Douglas, Madame C. J. Walker, the Tuskegee Airmen, Rosa Parks, Martin Luther King Jr., Malcolm X to Barack Obama, our history is rich.

From Jim Crow to Civil Rights to the Black Panthers, to the Watts Riots, and the Jena Six, our history is rich.

From Muddy Waters to Ella Fitzgerald, Shirley Caesar, Leontyne Price, Patti Labelle, The Clark Sisters, to Beyoncé, our history is rich.

From W. E.B. Dubois to Thurgood Marshall, Adam Clayton Powell, Barbara Jordan, Shirley Chisholm, Clarence Thomas, to Johnnie Cochran, our history is rich.

From Lena Horne to Ozzie Davis and Ruby Dee to Denzel Washington and Tyler Perry, our history is rich.

From Joe Lewis to Muhammad Ali, Michael Jordan, Lisa Leslie, Serena and Venus Williams, to Tiger Woods, our history is rich.

From Baptist, First AME, Methodist, Presbyterian, to Church of God in Christ, our history is rich.

Our history has shaped us and defined our place in America's history. Some would ask how we made it and the answer is very simple. Our history is rich but our faith is even greater. Our spirituality, our belief in a greater power has sustained us and has made us a people who can survive the test of times. Perhaps our ancestors kept Hebrews 11:1 in their spirit: Faith is the substance of things hoped for, the evidence of things not seen.

Let us not forget that we have history because first there was HIStory. Let us not forget that we serve an awesome God. Let us not forgot that He was born in a manger and He paid the price on Calvary.

Our ancestors prayed through unimaginable tribulations and taught their children, and their children taught their children to utter the name of Jesus in times of trouble and triumph. Our ancestors knew when they were weak He was strong.

When they cried out, He wiped every tear from their eyes. When they could not walk, He carried them. When they prayed, He answered their prayers and supplied all of their needs. Throughout history, God has been with us every step of the way and He will continue to be with us, and generations to come, because we have more work to do. Let us not forget from where we come from, for our history is rich.

Thank you all for coming. Now let's cut this ribbon, take a tour and celebrate what God has done for this community."

The audience roared with an overbearing thunderous applause.

The kids rushed to the podium and we shared in a group hug. Clark handed me the scissors and I cut the ribbon. Visions of Beauty, was officially open.

Moses' voice rumbled through the microphone. "May I have your attention please, just for a moment if everyone can stop and listen before we begin the tour. I need Unique to return to the podium."

I was bewildered. There was nothing left to do. We had covered all the pomp and circumstance. It was time to start the tours and more importantly it was time to eat. I had starved all week so I would look cute in my Vera Wang. I slowly and cautiously walked to Moses' side. He was grinning from ear to ear.

"Ladies and gentlemen, over the past two and a half years I have worked with Unique on this project and I have grown to love and respect her. She is an incredible, caring, compassionate human being who adores her children but most importantly she loves God. She means the world to me. I have waited a lifetime to find the one God created specifically for me."

Moses got down on bended knee. The kids, Netta, Angel, Ruby and Char surrounded us. Moses continued to speak.

"Unique, if you would have me I want to spend the rest of my life with you. Please say yes and honor me by accepting this proposal and becoming my wife."

He pulled out a stunning Emerald cut diamond, in a platinum setting. I stood there with my mouth gapped open. Clark whispered in my ear, "Surrender all and be blessed."

I shouted at the top of my lungs, "Yes! Yes! I'll marry you."

Pastor Rollins stepped up to the mike, "Well there's no time like the present and I just happen to have a marriage license. What do you say Unique?"

"How did you get one without me?"

Pastor Rollins laughed and looked at Angel. "I have my connections."

"Well, what do you say?" Moses asked me and whispered in my ear, "I've waited two and a half years to make love to you. Don't make me wait another day."

I giggled. "Okay, let's get married."

"Dearly, beloved…"

The End

CPSIA information can be obtained
at www.ICGtesting.com
Printed in the USA
LVOW04s1819111115
462088LV00030B/804/P